CRO
24-H

A cut
Fully equip

Crocodile Creek's state-of-the-art Medical
Centre and Rescue Response Unit is home to a
team of expertly trained medical professionals.
These dedicated men and women face the
challenges of life, love and medicine every day!

An abandoned baby!
The tension is mounting as a new-born baby
is found in the Outback whilst a young girl
fights for her life.

Two feuding families!
A long-held rivalry is threatening the well-being
of the community. Only hospital head Charles
Wetherby holds the key to this bitter battle.

A race to save lives!
Crocodile Creek's highly skilled medical rescue
team must compete with the fierce heat of the
Australian Outback and the scorching power
of their own emotions.

**HIS SECRET LOVE-CHILD is the first of four
continuing stories from Marion Lennox, Alison
Roberts, Lilian Darcy and Meredith Webber.
Join them at Crocodile Creek every month
in Mills & Boon® Medical Romance™**

Dear Reader

As many of you know, I'm from Australia, home of Truly Scary Wildlife. I write fiction, but sometimes real life is scarier.

Some months ago, an extended family camped by one of our northern rivers. During the night a crocodile entered one of the family tents and grabbed a young father. Crocs don't mess around. Once a croc has you, there's little you can do to fight back. When the croc started dragging the young man towards the river he knew what his fate would be, but as he was dragged away he screamed to his wife to save the baby.

But the croc reckoned without Grandma. Grandma woke, assumed the croc had the baby, and promptly jumped on its head. Despite being savagely bitten, despite her arm being broken, she stayed where she was until someone found a gun.

Everyone lived to tell the tale.

This wonderful true story led to four of us Down Under authors thinking what a fantastic setting the harsh north of Australia would be for a story—or a bunch of stories. We thought about the men and women of the Outback Medivac services and what drama they see every day of their working lives. The idea of **CROCODILE CREEK: 24-HOUR RESCUE** was born.

So... What better way to start a series than with an abandoned baby and a house full of medical rescue personnel; young doctors from around the world finding excitement and passion—oh, and crocodiles?

I've loved writing my **Crocodile Creek** story. I hope you love reading it, and that you'll follow us as we take you to our exciting fact-meets-fiction world.

Marion Lennox

HIS SECRET LOVE-CHILD

BY
MARION LENNOX

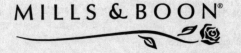

MILLS & BOON®

First published in Great Britain 2006
Harlequin Mills & Boon Limited,
Eton House, 18-24 Paradise Road, Richmond, Surrey TW9 1SR

© Marion Lennox 2006

ISBN 0 263 84716 0

Set in Times Roman 10½ on 12 pt.
03-0306-51425

Printed and bound in Spain
by Litografia Rosés, S.A., Barcelona

CHAPTER ONE

THIS old house had seen it all.

He should find somewhere else to live, Cal decided as he sat on the back veranda and gazed out over the moonlit sea. Living in a house filled with young doctors from every corner of the world could sometimes be a riot, but sometimes it was just plain scary.

Like now. Kirsty-the-Intern and Simon-the-Cardiologist had disappeared into the sunset, protesting personal concerns so serious they needed to break their contracts. They'd left a house agog with gossip, two bereft lovers and a hospital that was desperately understaffed.

Crocodile Creek, Remote Rescue Base, for all of far north Queensland, was notoriously short of doctors at the best of times. Two doctors were away on leave, a third had somersaulted his bike last week and was still in traction, and a fourth—unbelievably—had chickenpox. The two doctors who'd left so hastily hadn't considered that when they'd started their hot little…personal concern.

Dammit, Cal thought. Damn them. Now there was a bereft and confused Emily, and Mike, whose pride at least would be dented. Both were wonderful medics and fine friends. In such a confined household even Cal would be called on for comfort, and if there was one thing Dr Callum Jamieson disliked above all else, it was getting involved. All Cal wanted from life was to practise his medicine and commune with his beer.

And not think about Gina.

So why was he thinking of Gina now? It had been five years since he'd seen her. She should be forgotten.

She wasn't.

It was just this emotional stuff that was making him maudlin, he thought savagely. The old bush-nursing hospital that now served as Crocodile Creek's doctors' residence seemed to be a constant scene for some sort of emotional drama—and dramas made him think of Gina.

Gina walking away and not looking back.

He had to stop thinking of her! Gina had been his one dumb foray into emotional attachment and he was well out of it.

Maybe he should find Mike and play some pool, he thought. That'd clear his head of unwanted memories, it'd stop him swearing at the sea and maybe it'd help Mike.

But there wasn't time. He'd have to take another shift tonight. There might be no surgery to perform, but with the current shortage of doctors Cal could be called on to treat anything from hayfever to snake bite.

That meant he couldn't even have another beer.

Damn Simon. Damn Kirsty, he thought savagely. Their sordid little affair was messing with his life. His friends had loved them and he didn't want his friends to be unhappy. He wanted the Crocodile Creek doctors' house to be as it had been until today—a fun-filled house full of life and laughter, a place to base himself without care while he practised the medicine he loved.

The door opened and Emily, of the now non-existent Simon-and-Emily partnership, was standing behind him, pale-faced and tear-stained. Emily was a highly skilled anaesthetist. He and Emily made a great operating team.

Right now Emily looked about sixteen years old.

He didn't do emotional involvement!

But he moved on the ancient settee to let her sit beside him, and he put an arm around her and he hugged. OK, he didn't do emotional involvement but Emily was a sweetheart.

'Simon's a rat,' he told her.

'He's not.' She hiccuped on a sob. 'He'll come back. He and Kirsty aren't really—'

'He and Kirsty *are* really,' he told her. It wasn't helping anything if she kept deceiving herself. 'He really is a rat, and you can't love a rat. Think about the life they lead down there in the sewers. Gross. Come on, Em. You can do better than that.'

'Says you,' she whispered. 'You lost your lady-rat five years ago, and have you done better since Gina left? I don't think so.'

'Hey!' He was so startled he almost spilled his beer. How did Em know about Gina? Then he gave an inward groan. How could she not? Everyone knew everything in this dratted house. Sometimes he thought they were even privy to his dreams.

'We're not talking about me,' he said, trying to sound neutral. 'We're talking about you. You're the one who needs to recover from a broken heart.'

'Well, I'm not going to learn from you, then,' she wailed. 'Five years, and you're still not over it. Charles says you're just as much in love with Gina as you were five years ago, and for me it's just starting. Oh, Cal, I can't bear it.'

Gunyamurra. Three hundred miles south. A birth and then…a heartbeat?

No. It was her imagination. There was nothing.

Nothing.

Distressed beyond measure, the girl stared down at the tiny scrap of humanity that should have been her son. Maybe he could have been her son. Given another life.

How could she have hoped this child would live? She was little more than a child herself, so how could she have ever dared to dream? How could she have ever deserved something so wonderful as a baby?

Now what? Living, this child might well have made her life explode into meaning. But now…

It would all go on as before, the girl thought drearily. Somehow.

Her body ached with physical pain and desolate loss. She was weighed down, sinking already back into the thick, grey abyss of the last few months' despair.

She put out a tentative finger and traced the contours of the lifeless face. Her baby.

She had to leave him. There was no use in her staying, and this quiet place of moss and ferns was as good a place as any to say goodbye.

'I wish your father could have seen you,' she whispered, and at the thought of what might have been, the tears finally started to flow.

Tears were useless. She had to get back. The cars were leaving. She'd slip into the back seat of the family car and her parents wouldn't even question where she'd been. They wouldn't notice.

Of course they wouldn't notice. Why would they? Her life was nothing.

Her baby was dead.

'There's a baby behind my rock.'

Gina closed her eyes in frustration and tried hard not to snap. CJ's need for the toilet was turning into a marathon. The coach left the rodeo grounds in ten minutes and if they missed the coach…

They couldn't miss the coach. Being stranded at Gunyamurra in the heart of Australia's Outback was the stuff of nightmares.

'CJ, just do what you need to do and come on out,' she ordered, trying hard for a voice with inbuilt authority. It didn't work. Dr Gina Lopez might be a highly qualified cardiologist who worked in a state-of-the-art medical unit back home in the US, but controlling one four-year-old was sometimes beyond her.

CJ was just like his daddy, she thought wearily. Even though those big brown eyes made her heart melt, he was fiercely independent, determined to follow his own road, whatever the cost.

Like now. CJ had taken one look at the portable toilets and dug in his heels.

'I'm not using them. They're horrible.'

They were, too, Gina conceded. The Gunyamurra Rodeo had come to an end, the portable toilets had accommodated a couple of hundred beer-swilling patrons and CJ's criticism was definitely valid.

So she'd directed his small person to where the parking lot turned into bushland. Even then she had problems. Her independent four-year-old required privacy.

'Someone will see me.'

'Go behind a rock. No one will see.'

'OK, but I'm going behind the rock by myself.'

'Fine.'

And now...

'There's a baby behind my rock.'

Right. She loved his imagination but this was no time for dreaming.

'CJ, please, hurry,' she told him, with another anxious glance across the parking lot where the coach was almost ready to leave. She was too far away to call out, and she hadn't told the driver to wait. If they missed the coach...

Stop panicking, she told herself. It'd come this way. If the worst came to the worst, she could step down into its path and stop it. She might irritate the driver but that was the least of her problems.

She should never have come here, she thought wearily. It had been stupid.

But it had seemed necessary.

Back in the States she'd thought maybe, just maybe she could find the courage to face Cal. Maybe she could find the courage to tell him what he eventually had to know.

But now she was even questioning that need. Was it even fair to tell him?

She'd started out with the best of intentions. She'd arrived at Crocodile Creek late last Thursday and she'd left CJ with her landlady so she could go to find him. The house she'd been directed to was the doctors' quarters—a rambling old house on a bluff overlooking the sea. At dusk it had looked beautiful. The setting should have given her courage.

It hadn't. By the time she'd reached the house, her heart had been in her boots. Then, when no one had answered her knock, things had become even worse.

She'd walked around the side of the house and there he'd been, on the veranda. Cal. The Cal she remembered from all those years, with all her heart.

But he wasn't her Cal. Of course he wasn't. Time had moved on. He hadn't seen her, and then, just as she had been forcing herself to call his name, a young woman had come out of the house to join him.

Gina had stilled, sinking back into the shadows, and a moment later she had been desperately glad she had. Because Cal had taken the woman into his arms. His face had been in her hair, he had whispered softly, and as Gina had stood there, transfixed, the woman's arms had come around Cal's shoulders to embrace him back.

This wasn't passion, Gina thought as she watched them. Maybe if it had seemed like passion she could still have done what she'd intended. But this was more. It was a coming together of two people who needed each other. There was something about the way they held each other that said their relationship was deep and real. The girl's face looked pinched and wan. Cal cupped her chin in his hand and he forced her eyes to meet his, and Gina's heart twisted in a pain so fierce she almost cried out. This girl had found what she never had.

She'd fled. Of course she'd fled. She'd treated Cal so appallingly in the past. Now it seemed that he'd found love. Real love—the sort of love they'd never shared. What right did she have to interfere with him now?

She'd gone back to her hotel, cuddled CJ and tried to regroup, but the more she thought about it the more impossible it seemed. How would Cal's lady react to her appearing on the scene? How could she jeopardise this relationship for him?

She couldn't. CJ had been born in wedlock. Paul was his father and that was the way it had to stay.

But she'd invested so much. She'd come so far. Surely she couldn't simply take the next plane home, though that was what she frantically wanted to do.

She'd promised CJ they'd see Australia. She had to make good that promise.

So she'd made herself wait a few days. She'd booked herself and her young son onto a crocodile hunt—a search by moonlight for the great creatures that inhabited the local estuaries. Thy hadn't found a crocodile but they'd met a real live crocodile hunter and CJ's wide-eyed enjoyment of his stories had helped ease the ache in her heart. They'd taken a tour out to the Great Barrier Reef and had tried not to be disappointed when the weather had been wild and the water cloudy.

Then she'd heard about the Gunyamurra Rodeo. CJ's passion was for horses. There'd been a coach going via the rodeo to the airport, and the last day of the rodeo was a short one, so they'd decided to spend their last morning in Australia here.

CJ had loved it, so maybe it hadn't been a total waste of time, but now the thought of leaving was overwhelmingly appealing. Crocodile Creek was three hundred miles away. She was never going to see Cal again. Their coach was due to leave to take them back to Cairns Airport, and it was over.

All she had to do was get her son from behind his rock.

'CJ, hurry.'

'I can't do anything here,' he told her with exaggerated patience. 'There's a baby.'

'There's no baby.'

CJ's imagination was wonderful, Gina thought ruefully, and at any other time she encouraged it. Her son filled his life with imaginary friends, imaginary animals, rockets, battleships, babies. He saw them everywhere.

Not now. She couldn't indulge him now.

'There's not a baby,' she snapped again, and, dignity or not, she peered around CJ's rock.

There was a baby.

For a moment she was too stunned to move. She stood and stared at the place between two rocks—the place where her son was gazing.

This was a birth scene. One fast glance told her that. Someone had lain here and delivered a baby. The grass was crushed and there was blood…

And a baby.

A dead baby?

She moved swiftly, stooping to see, noting his stillness and the dreadful blue tinge of his skin. He was so pale under his waxy birth coating that she thought he must be dead.

She touched him and there was a hint of warmth.

Warmth? Maybe.

He wasn't breathing.

She fell to her knees and lifted him against her. His tiny body was limp and floppy. Where was his pulse?

Nothing.

Her fingers were in his mouth, trying frantically to clear an airway that was far too small. She turned him over, face down, using her little finger to clear muck from his mouth and then using a fold of her T-shirt to wipe his mouth clear.

Then she pulled him up to her mouth and breathed.

She felt his tiny chest lift.

Yes!

Heartbeat. Come on. There had to be a heartbeat.

Her backpack was where she'd dropped it, and CJ's windcheater was drooping out of the top. She hauled it onto the grass and laid the baby down on its soft surface. It was almost one movement, spreading the windcheater, laying the little one down and starting cardiopulmonary resuscitation.

She knew this so well. Cardiology was her specialty but to practise CPR here, on a baby this small...

She wanted her hospital. She wanted oxygen and suction equipment. She wanted back-up.

She had to find help. Even if she got him breathing, she needed help. Urgently.

CJ was standing, stunned into silence. He was too young to depend on but he was all she had.

'CJ, run to the side of the parking lot and scream for help,' she told him between breaths.

Breathe, press, press, press...

'Why?' CJ seemed totally bemused, and who could blame him?

Could she take the baby and run for help? She rejected the idea almost before she thought of doing it. How long had the baby been abandoned? How long had he not been breathing? Even if she got him back... Every second without oxygen increased the chance of brain damage.

She needed every ounce of concentration to get air into these little lungs. She breathed again into the baby's mouth and continued with the rhythmic pumping that must get the heart working. Must!

'This baby's really ill,' she told CJ, fighting to get words out as she concentrated on CPR between breaths 'You have to get someone to come here. Scream like there's a tiger chasing you.'

'There's not a tiger.'

'Pretend there is.' She was back to breathing again. Then: 'Go, CJ. I need your help. You have to scream.'

'For the baby?'

'For the baby.'

He considered for a long moment. Then he nodded as if he'd decided that maybe that what his mother was asking wasn't too crazy. Maybe it even appealed to him. He disappeared around the other side of the rock. There was a moment's silence—and then a yell.

'Tiger. Tiger. Tiger. There's a tiger and a baby. *Help!*'

It was a great yell. It was the best. He'd put his heart into it, and it sounded for all the world like a tiger was about to pounce, and a baby, too. But the end of his yell was drowned out.

The coach they'd come in was huge, a two-level touring affair. It had a massive air-conditioning unit, and even when idling it was noisy. Now, as it started to move and went through its ponderous gear changes, it was truly deafening.

Gina heard just one of CJ's yells before the sound of the coach took over. The second and third yells were drowned out as the coach turned out of the parking lot, growing louder and louder until nothing could be heard at all.

Gina made to stand—she made to get herself out in front of the coach to stop it—but then there was a tiny choking sound from the baby. Her eyes flew back to him. Was she imagining it?

No.

If he was choking… His airway must still be slightly blocked. She had to get his trachea clear.

Once more she lifted the baby and turned him face down, and her fingers searched his mouth. The coach was forgotten. She desperately needed equipment. There might well be liquor or meconium stuck in his throat or on his vocal cords. How to clear his tiny airway without tracheal suction?

She shook him, carefully, carefully, supporting his neck as if it were the most precious thing in the world.

He choked again.

Something dislodged—a fragment of gunk—and she had it clear in an instant.

She turned him back over and breathed for him again.

This time his chest rose higher.

It fell.

It rose—all by itself.

Again.

Again.

She was breathing with him, willing him to breathe with her. And he was. Wonderfully—magically—he was.

She wiped his mouth again, using her T-shirt, and then searched her bag for a facecloth. She was cradling him against her now. She had to get him warm. Once she had him breathing, heat loss was his biggest enemy.

At least the outside air was warm.

She had to get help.

The coach was gone.

As if on cue, CJ appeared back from his tiger yelling. 'I think they heard me,' he told her, uncertain whether to be proud or not. His expression said he was definitely uncertain about the baby his mother was paying such attention to. 'One of the ladies on the coach waved to me as it went past.'

Fantastic. She could hear it in the distance, rumbling down the unmade road, starting its long trip to Cairns.

To the airport. To America. Home.

She couldn't think of that now. All that mattered was this tiny baby. His breathing was becoming less laboured, she thought, or was it wishful thinking? She wanted oxygen so badly.

She didn't have it. She had to concentrate on the things she could do.

Swiftly she checked the baby's umbilical cord. It looked as if it had been ripped from the placenta. Now that his heart was beating strongly, the cord was starting to ooze.

How long had the cord been cut? she asked herself, a bit confused. Obstetrics wasn't her strong point, but surely the cord shouldn't still be bleeding?

How much blood had he lost?

Where was the nearest hospital to Gunyamurra?

She couldn't depend on a hospital. She was all this baby had.

She tugged the drawstring from her backpack and tied the umbilicus with care, then hauled the backpack wide and found her own windcheater—a soft, old garment that she loved. It'd do as a blanket.

Once again she checked his breathing, scarcely allowing herself to hope that this frail little scrap of humanity might survive.

But as if he'd read her mind and was determined to prove her wrong, he opened his eyes.

And even CJ was caught.

'It's a real baby,' CJ breathed, awed at this transformation from what must have seemed a lifeless body to a living thing, and Gina could only gaze down at the baby in her arms and agree.

More. There were no words for this moment. For this miracle. She was suddenly holding a little person in her arms. A baby boy. A child who'd one day grow to be a man, because CJ had found him and her lifesaving techniques had blessedly worked.

How could missing a coach possibly compare to this? How could being stuck in this outlandish place possibly matter?

He was so tiny. Four, maybe five pounds? Premature? He had to be. His fingernails had scarcely started to form and he was so small.

His lips were still tinged with blue. Cyanosis? The tips of his fingers were still blue as well, and she started to worry all over again. As he'd started to breathe, his little body had suffused with colour, but now…

She checked his fingers and toes with care, trying not to expose him any more than she had to. It was a hot day, so the wind was warm against the baby's skin. How long had he been exposed?

Maybe the warm wind had helped save his life.

But there were still those worrying traces of cyanosis. His heart wasn't working at a hundred per cent.

It wasn't his breathing, she thought. He was gazing up, wide-eyed, as if wondering where on earth he was, and his breathing seemed to be settling.

So why the skin blueness?

She wanted medical back-up. She wanted it now.

'How will we get home?' CJ asked, and she held the baby close and tried to make herself think.

'We need to find someone to help us.'

'Everyone's gone,' CJ said.

'Surely not everyone.'

But maybe everyone had. Gina's heart sank. The rodeo itself had finished almost an hour ago. A group of country and western musicians from down on the coast had booked the coach to transport their gear. They'd played at the closing ceremony, then organised the coach to stay longer, giving them time to pack up.

The timing meant that the crowd had dispersed. The rodeo had taken place miles from the nearest settlement—which itself wasn't much of a settlement. There'd been mobile food vans and a mobile pub, but they'd gone almost before the last event.

CJ might well be right.

'Someone must be here,' she said, trying to sound assured. She tucked the baby underneath her T-shirt, against her skin, hoping the warmth of her skin would do the same job as an incubator. 'Come on, CJ. Let's go find someone.'

CJ was looking at her as if he wasn't quite sure whether he wanted to accompany her or not. 'Is the baby OK?'

'I think so.' She hoped so.

'You've got blood on your shirt.'

She had. She grimaced down at her disgusting T-shirt but she wasn't thinking of her appearance. She was thinking of how much blood the baby had lost.

Why had he bled so much? And newborn babies had so little... He couldn't afford to have lost this much.

He whimpered a little against her and she felt a tiny surge of reassurance. And something more.

Once upon a time—four and a half years ago—she'd held CJ like this, and she'd made the vows she found were forming again in her heart right now. She'd loved CJ's daddy so much. Cal had taught her what loving could be, and she'd pass that loving on to CJ.

And even though Cal no longer came into it—even though Cal was no part of her life and had nothing to do with this baby—she found herself voicing those same vows. She'd protect this baby, come what may.

What mother could have left him here? she wondered. How much trouble must a woman be suffering to drag herself away from her newborn child?

She thought of how distressed she'd been when CJ had been born—how much she'd longed for Cal and how impossible it had seemed that she raise her son without him. But the bond to her tiny scrap of a son had been unbreakable, regardless.

He'd been her link to Cal.

She'd thought of Cal so much as her son had been born, and suddenly, achingly, she thought of him now.

But it was crazy. She couldn't think of Cal. Neither could she think about the coach growing further away by the minute. Her ticket out of here—away from Cal for ever—was gone.

She needed to find help.

'Come on, CJ. There must be someone still around.' She cradled the baby with one hand, took CJ's hand with the other and went to find out.

The rodeo had been held in a natural arena where a ring of hills formed a natural showground. There was scrub and bush-land on the hills but the rodeo ground was a huge, dusty area that now looked barren and deserted.

But not everyone had gone. As Gina and CJ crossed the parking lot back into the rodeo grounds, they found one sol-itary person—an elderly, native Australian. Gina had seen him before, working on the sidelines during the rodeo. Was he some sort of ground manager? He must be. He was star-ing around at the piles of litter and scratching his head in dis-gust. As he saw Gina and CJ, he shoved back his hat and smiled, obviously pleased to be distracted from the mess.

'G'day. Come to help me clean up?'

'We've found a baby,' Gina told him.

He stared. His smile faded.

'Um…say again?'

'Someone has abandoned a baby in the bush. I have him here.' She motioned to the bulge beneath her stained T-shirt. 'We need medical help. Fast.'

'You'll be kidding me.'

'I'm not joking.' She outlined what had happened and the man's jaw dropped almost to his ankles.

'You're saying some woman just dropped her bundle be-hind the rocks—and left it for dead?'

'She may have thought he was dead already,' Gina told him. 'I had trouble getting him to breathe.'

The man cast an uneasy glance at the bulge under her shirt. He took a step back, as if maybe he was facing a lunatic. 'So he's under there? A baby.'

'He's under there. Can you take us to the nearest hospital?'

The man stared at her for a moment longer, took another step backward and then motioned uncertainly to an ancient truck parked nearby.

'There's no other way of getting out of here than that. How did you get here?'

'Coach.'

'The coach has left.'

'Yes,' Gina said, trying to hold her impatience in check. 'Will you take us to the hospital? We need help.'

'Nearest clinic's at Gunyamurra, twenty miles from here,' he told her, still really doubtful. 'But there's no one there now. The Wetherbys and the Gunnings—the two families that live near there and the workers on their stations—they were all here today so there won't be a clinic operating. Maybe you need a doctor.'

'Yes, please.' To tell him she was a doctor herself would only confuse matters.

He cast another glance at her bulge. His mouth tightened as if he was becoming sure of his lunatic theory.

'How can I contact medical help?' she snapped, and he blinked.

'We had the Remote Rescue Service on call during the rodeo,' he told her, totally bemused. 'They flew Joseph Long out with a broken leg an hour or so back. That was near the end with only the novelty events left, so they didn't come back. Word is that they're short a couple of doctors back at base.'

'I need a doctor now,' Gina told him. She was still holding

CJ's hand tight and using her other hand to cradle the baby. But the baby didn't seem to be moving. He was so limp.

He couldn't die. He mustn't.

'I s'pose I could call them back.' There was another doubtful look at her bloodstained T-shirt—a look that said he accepted there was blood and maybe there had been a baby but he wasn't too sure that he mightn't be dealing with an axe murderer. 'You sure it really is a baby? A live baby?'

She released CJ and held up the T-shirt—just for a moment, just so he could see.

They all looked at the bulge.

At the windcheater-wrapped baby.

He was surely real. He was surely a baby. He was incredibly tiny—more, he was incredibly beautiful. His crumpled little face was now becoming the flushed crimson of most newborns. His eyes were wide, dazed and unfocussed.

And he moved. It was a slight movement, but he definitely moved. He whimpered a little and a hand—a hand the size of a man's fingernail—broke free from his makeshift blanket.

Gina didn't say anything. She tucked the little hand back into the warmth of her windcheater, and she waited for this man to make his decision. She needed his help so much.

And it seemed that she had it. The man stared down and his face twisted into an expression she could scarcely read,

'Will you look at that?' he whispered. 'He's just like mine were at that age.' He stared down at the baby for a moment longer and then he looked up at Gina. His old eyes met hers and held.

'You really found him?'

'We found him. We're tourists on the coach but we found him just as the coach was leaving. I've been trying to get him to breathe. So far, so good, but if he's to live we need your help. We need outside help. Fast.'

'I'm moving,' he told her, and he turned and started to stride swiftly across the dusty arena to his truck.

He took three long strides—and then he started to run.

'Mommy,' CJ said, in the tone of a patient man whose patience was being tested to the limit.

'Yes?'

'I still need to go to the toilet.'

'Cal?'

He jumped. Cal had been placing a scalpel in the steriliser, but Charles's voice from right behind him startled him into dropping it. He swore, then stooped to retrieve it with a sigh. 'Will you cut that out?' he demanded of his boss. 'Quit oiling that damned wheelchair so we have a chance.'

Charles grinned. Charles Wetherby was the medical director of Crocodile Creek Medical Centre. He'd been confined to a wheelchair since a shooting accident when he'd been eighteen, but his paraplegia didn't stop him being a fine doctor and a medical director who missed nothing. Charles knew his silent approaches startled his staff but he didn't mind. It never hurt his young doctors to believe their medical director might be right beside them at any time.

Not that he had any need to check on Cal. Callum Jamieson was one of the best doctors they'd ever been blessed with.

Normally doctors didn't stay at Crocodile Creek for too long. The work was hard, the place was one of the most remote in the world and doctors tended to treat it almost as a mission. They spent a couple of years here working with the Remote Rescue team, they got their need for excitement out of their system and then they disappeared.

Not Cal. He'd come four years ago and had made no attempt to move. There was something holding him, Charles had decided long before this. Something that didn't make him want to face the real world. Woman trouble? Charles didn't know for sure what the whole story was, but he knew more than Cal ever admitted—and he'd met Gina. For now, though, he wasn't asking questions. Cal was a fine surgeon, and he went that extra step with patients. He really cared. Also, Cal was more gentle and painstaking with the indigenous people than any of the younger doctors who struggled with—and often didn't care about—their culture. Cal was invaluable to this Remote Rescue Service and Charles was deeply grateful that he had him.

Especially now.

'I need you in the chopper,' he told him.

'Trouble?'

'Out at the rodeo.'

'Didn't Christina and Mike just bring someone in?'

'Yeah. Joseph Long, with a fractured femur. You'd think kids would have something better to do than to risk life and limb sitting on a steer that doesn't want to be sat on.'

'How old were you when you got shot pig-shooting?' Cal asked mildly. 'Eighteen? Don't tell me. Joseph's…what? Eighteen? You're telling me that kids should learn a lesson from you and stop being risk-takers?'

'Don't play the moral bit on me.' Charles's craggy features twisted into a wry grin. There weren't many people who could joke with Charles about his background, but Cal had been around long enough to become a firm friend. 'Just get on that chopper,' he told him. 'Fast.'

'What's up.'

'Newborn. Breathing difficulties.'

Cal came close to dropping his scalpel again. 'A newborn at the rodeo?'

'There's a woman there says she found him.'

'A woman?'

'Hey, I don't know any more than you do,' Charles said, exasperated. 'I know it sounds crazy and if I could, I'd be in the air right now, finding out what's going on. But Pete Sargent—the rodeo groundsman—has radioed in, saying there's a baby and a woman and for some reason they don't match. He says the woman found the baby. The baby's certainly in trouble and he wants a doctor out there fast. Mike's refuelling the chopper as we speak. You're the only doctor available. So what are you standing here for?'

Gina was just about frantic.

The blue tinge to the baby's fingertips and lips was becoming more and more pronounced. Cyanosis in a newborn had to mean heart trouble—but she didn't even have a stethoscope. She was sitting in the rodeo judges' stall and as a hospital ward it made a great judges' stall. There was no equipment whatsoever.

Pete—bless him—had taken CJ in charge. Out on the grounds the pair of them were collecting litter. Pete had supplied CJ with a pair of work-gloves that were longer than his arms, and CJ was enjoying himself immensely.

That left Gina free to concentrate on the baby, but there was so little she could do. She kept his airway clear. She watched his breathing. She kept him against her skin, curving in so he had as much skin contact as possible, cradling any exposed parts into her soft, old windcheater. She was using herself as an incubator.

She willed him to live, and she waited.

Help came so slowly she thought she might well lose him.

But finally the helicopter came in from the east, low and fast and loud. It hovered for a moment above the car park as if the pilot was checking for obstacles. But Pete had already checked. There was no problem with its landing, and before it reached the ground Gina was running toward it.

She stopped just out of range of the rotor blades. Pete had come up behind her. The elderly groundsman was holding

CJ's hand and he gripped her arm, too, as if warning her that the rotor was dangerous.

Maybe he still thought she was deranged, Gina decided. He must think there was a possibility she might run into the blades.

She wouldn't. She knew about helicopters. She'd flown with the Remote Rescue Service before.

So she stood and she waited, but she didn't have long to wait. A man was emerging from the passenger seat, his long body easing out onto the gravel. He hauled a bag out after him, then turned.

Her world stopped.

Cal.

CHAPTER TWO

FOR how long had she dreamed of this moment? For how long had she thought of what she might say?

Her prepared speech was no longer appropriate. She'd accepted that three nights ago when she'd seen him back at Crocodile Creek, so maybe it was just as well that there were things to say and do now that had nothing to do with their past.

He was past the slowing rotor blades. He was almost by her side.

He stopped.

And he saw who he was facing.

'Gina.'

The word was a blank expression of pure shock.

He'd had less warning than she. She at least knew that he was in the same part of the world as she was. She'd seen him only three days ago. But Cal hadn't seen her for five years.

He'd hardly changed, she thought. He was a big man, long and lean and tough. He always had been.

Information about Cal's background had been hard to glean, but she knew enough. His parents had been farmers on a holding that had been scarcely viable. His mother had abandoned them early. Cal had been brought up to hard times and hard work, and it showed. His bronzed skin was weathered, almost leathery. His deep brown eyes crinkled at the edges, and his strongly boned face spoke of the childhood he'd talked about reluctantly, a childhood where his first memory had been of gathering hay in the blazing sun before a storm on Christmas morning, heaving bales that had been almost as big as he'd been before he had been old enough to stop believing in Santa Claus.

Before he'd been old enough to stop hoping that one day things could change.

But they hadn't. He hadn't. He hadn't changed a bit.

Yet she still loved him. She looked into his shocked face and she felt her heart break all over again.

How could she still love him?

Five years of heartbreak.

She had to move on. He had a life to lead and so did she. There was no room here for emotion.

But... His burnt red, tightly curled hair was just the same as her son's.

Concentrate on medicine, she told herself fiercely. Use the medical imperative. Medicine had been her lifesaver for five long years and it would be her lifesaver again.

And as for loving?

Get over it.

'Cal, there's a baby.'

He was staring at her as if he were seeing a ghost. She might be moving on, but he hadn't yet. How could he?

'What the hell are you doing here?'

The harsh words were like a blow and she found herself physically flinching.

But she had to move past this. The baby's life was too important to waste time on non-essentials.

'I've been at the rodeo,' she told him. Somehow. It was almost impossible to make her voice work at all, but when she managed it came out expressionless. Businesslike. 'I found a baby,' she managed.

'You found a baby.' Shock was still the overriding emotion.

'It's wrapped in a windcheater, under her T-shirt.' Pete had moved into helpful mode now. He was looking from Gina to Cal and back again, as if he couldn't figure out why they weren't moving. As indeed they must. 'She says some woman must have dropped it in the bush.'

'What—?'

'I need oxygen,' Gina told him, hauling herself even more into medical mode and willing Cal to follow. 'Cal, the baby needs urgent help if he's to survive. He's badly cyanosed. His breathing is way too shallow—he's tiring while I watch.'

She still hadn't pulled the baby from under her T-shirt so he was just a bulge under her bloodstained clothing. No wonder she didn't have Cal's belief. She must look crazy. 'He's only hours old. He's lost blood. He's prem, I think, and he's not perfusing as he should. Blue lips, blue fingernails. Heartbeat seems far too rapid. Do you have equipment?'

She watched as Cal caught himself. As he finally managed to flick an internal switch.

'A baby.' His eyes dropped to the bulge and his deep eyes widened. He was taking in the whole scene, and it wasn't pretty. 'Not yours?'

'Not mine.' A little blood could go a long way and she was aware that she looked so gory she might well be a mother who'd given birth only hours before. And maybe she looked shocked and pale to go with it.

'I need oxygen, and I need it fast.'

'We have an incubator on board. Everything we need.' The pilot of the chopper—a guy in a flight suit—was coming toward them now, carrying more equipment.

Medical mode won.

'Let's move.'

* * *

They moved.

The next ten minutes were spent working as once they'd worked together long ago. The pilot—a youngish guy Cal referred to as Mike—was a paramedic and he was good, but with a baby this tiny they needed every ounce of skill they all possessed.

She and Cal were still a team, Gina thought fleetingly as she searched for and found a tiny vein for the intravenous drip. Newborn babies had such a tiny amount of blood that even a small loss could be catastrophic. He had to have replacement fluid. Meanwhile, Cal had a paediatric mask over the tiny face, using the attached bag to assist breathing. His breathing slowed almost at once. From an abandoned baby with nothing, this little one was suddenly being attached to every conceivable piece of medical technology they could use.

Maybe he'd need them all. Because when Cal hooked him to the heart monitor and she watched his heart rate, she winced.

'There's something going on,' she murmured. 'That heartbeat's too fast and with this level of cyanosis…'

'You're thinking maybe pulmonary stenosis?'

'Maybe. Or something worse, God forbid. We need an echocardiogram.'

'Yeah.' He cast her a doubtful look. 'We've done all we can here. We need to get him back to the base.'

She hesitated. Yes. They needed to get the baby to help. But…where did that leave her?

For the first time since she'd found the baby, there was a tiny sliver of time to consider. The baby was being warmed and he was hooked to oxygen and an intravenous drip. He was as stable as she could make him—for now. Somehow she made herself block out the fact that Cal was watching her as she forced herself to think through what should happen next.

Should she stay involved?

Now was the time to step back—if she could.

There were three factors coming into play here.

First, she badly needed transport. Once she reached Crocodile Creek, she could get a coach to the outside world. Maybe she could even still catch her flight home.

Secondly, more importantly, this baby needed her. Or he needed someone with specialist training.

'Is there a cardiologist at Crocodile Creek?' she asked, and Cal shook his head. He was thinking exactly what she was thinking. She knew it.

'Our cardiologist has just left,' he said abruptly, and she nodded. But the way he'd spoken… It brought her to the third factor.

Despite the fact that it was sensible for her to go with him to Crocodile Creek—despite the fact that medical imperative decreed that she go—she didn't want to get in the helicopter with him. It had been a mistake to come. To drag out the moment…

This baby needed a cardiologist if he was to survive. He needed her.

She had no choice, she told herself fiercely. Focus on medicine. Ignore the personal. The personal was all just too hard.

'We need to think about the mother,' she managed, and Cal nodded in agreement. They'd always been apt to follow the same train of thought and it was happening all over again.

'We do.' He turned away to where Pete was kneeling a few yards away in the dust. Pete had obviously decided that his best role was in keeping CJ occupied and they were etching huge drawings of kangaroos in the dust. 'Pete, have you no idea where this baby could possibly have come from?'

'There's been three or four hundred people through here over the last couple of days,' Pete said, looking up from his kangaroo and shaking his head as he thought it through. 'It could be anyone's kid.'

'This baby was born here only hours ago. Did you see anyone who was obviously pregnant?'

'Dorothy Curtin's got a bulge bigger'n a walrus but she and Max took off with the kids at lunch time.'

'There's no way Dorothy would abandon one of hers. But anyone else? Maybe someone who's in trouble. A kid? Maybe someone who's not a local?'

'There were a few out-of-towners on the coach. But I dunno.' He scratched his head a bit and thought about it. 'I dunno.'

'I didn't see any pregnant women on the bus,' Gina told them.

'I'll need to get the police involved.' Cal looked uncertainly across at Gina and then he seemed to make a decision. 'I want the mother found. But we need to take Gina—this lady—back to Crocodile Creek with us,' he told Pete. 'Will you stay on and show the police where the baby was found?'

'Sure thing,' Pete said. 'I gotta clean up anyway. '

'I'll show you exactly where I found her,' Gina told him, and then hesitated, thinking it through. 'Cal, we need to check the birth site anyway. We might have a girl somewhere who's in real trouble.'

'We might at that,' Cal said grimly—and then added, more enigmatically, 'And that's only the start of it.' He motioned to Mike. 'Mike, you go with Gina. I'll stay with the baby.'

Mike nodded. Until then the paramedic had worked almost silently alongside them, but he was obviously aware of undercurrents. He looked at Gina now, a long, assessing glance, and then he looked across to where CJ was intent on his drawing.

'Is this your son?' he asked her. 'Will he be coming back with us, too?'

Cal hadn't noticed CJ. He'd been preoccupied with the baby and with Gina, and CJ had had his head down, drawing dust pictures. Now his eyes jerked over to where the little boy knelt in the dust.

CJ was totally intent on the task at hand, as he was always intent on everything he did. Pete had been showing him the traditional way aboriginals depicted kangaroos and he was copying, dotting the spine of his kangaroo with tiny white pebbles. Each stone was being laid in order. His drawing of the kangaroo was three feet high—or three feet long—and it'd take many, many pebbles to complete it, but that wouldn't deter CJ.

So for now he knelt happily in the dust, a freckle-faced, skinny kid with a crop of burnt red curls that were coiled tight to his head. With deep brown eyes that flashed with intelligence.

With hair and with eyes that were just the same as his father's.

They all saw Cal's shock. Gina watched his eyes widen in incredulity. She could see him freeze. She could see the arithmetic going on in his head.

She could see his life change, as hers had changed with CJ's birth. Or maybe before that.

As it had changed the day she'd first met Cal.

'Hey, the kid's hair is just the same as yours,' Pete said easily—and then he fell silent. He, too, had sensed the tension that was suddenly almost palpable.

'It's great hair,' Mike said, with a long, hard stare at Cal. Then he recovered. A bit. 'OK.' He stared at CJ for another long moment—and then turned back to Gina. 'You said your name is Gina? I'm assuming you're a doctor?' Cal had been working with her as an equal and her medical training must have been obvious.

'That's right. I'm a cardiologist from the States.' But Gina was hardly concentrating on what she was saying. She was still watching Cal.

'Then let's get this birth site checked, shall we?' Mike said, taking charge because neither of the two doctors seemed capable of taking charge of anything. 'There are questions that need answers all over the place here.' He directed another long, hard stare at Cal—and then he took another look at CJ. 'So maybe we'd better start working on them right now.'

The flight back to Crocodile Creek was fast. They put CJ in the passenger seat next to Mike—helicopter copilot was a small boy's dream—and Gina and Cal were left in the back to tend to the baby.

But there was scarcely room for both of them to work, and for the moment there was little enough for both to do. It was Gina who opted out, Gina who sank into a seat and harnessed herself in for the ride and Gina who said, 'He's your patient, Cal.'

Which was fine, Cal thought as he monitored the little one, adjusting the oxygen rate, listening to the baby's heart, fighting to keep him stable.

The baby was his patient.

Gina's son was…was…

Hell, he couldn't take it in. It was overwhelming. The sight of the little boy had knocked him so hard he still felt as if he'd been punched.

How could Gina have borne a child—his child?—and not told him?

Could it be a mistake? Was he jumping to conclusions? Somewhere there was a husband. He knew that. A husband with coiled red hair the same as his? And eyes that looked like his?

He glanced across at Gina. She looked older, he thought. Much, much older than the last time he'd seen her.

He remembered the first time he'd seen her. She'd just arrived in Townsville, a young doctor from the States come to try her hand at Outback medicine. She'd been thin—almost too thin—her green eyes almost too big for her pinched, white face, and with her riot of deep brown curls tied back in a casual knot that had accentuated her pallor. He'd thought she seemed too young, too frail to take on the job she had applied for.

But over the year she'd been with the Remote Rescue

Service, she'd proved him wrong. She'd fast become an important member of the service. She gave her all. She'd thrown herself into her work with total enthusiasm and skill. With basic training in cardiology, she'd proved an indispensable member of their team, and the rest of the doctors had only been able to wonder what had driven her from her high-powered training to life in far north Queensland.

'I had a relationship that didn't work out. It was…a bit of a drama.' It was all anyone had been able to get from her. She didn't talk about her past.

But finally she did talk, though still not of her background. As they'd worked together over the ensuing months, the pinched, wan look had disappeared and she'd blossomed. She'd gained weight, her eyes had lost their haunted look and had filled with life and laughter, and she'd brought life and joy to…

To his world.

He'd thought her the most beautiful woman he'd ever seen.

He glanced again at her now. Her hands were clasped on her knees. She was staring straight ahead, unseeing.

She seemed haunted again, he thought. She was too damned thin again. The bloodstained clothes made her look like the victim of some disaster, and he had a sudden feeling that she'd look like that even without them.

He didn't know her, he thought bleakly. He had no idea what was happening behind that blank mask. She'd walked away from him five years ago and he hadn't seen her since. His only phone call had elicited a brutal response.

'I'm married, Cal. My husband needs me. Absolutely. I can't talk to you any more.'

Married. *Married.*

He needed to concentrate on his job. His fingers were lying lightly against the baby's neck, monitoring his vital signs by touch as well as by sight, but there was still time and still room for him to look at her again. She wasn't looking at him. She was staring down at her hands. She was wearing a plain gold wedding ring. Her fingers had clenched to white.

Why had she come?

Questions. There were questions everywhere. But for now only one mattered, he told himself.

Would this little one live?

He dragged his eyes away from Gina, back to the baby.

Needful or not, he'd continue to monitor him by sight, he decided. And by every other sense—because there was no way he could bear to look at Gina.

And he hardly dared to as much as glance at the little boy sitting next to Mike in the copilot's seat.

Questions. Too many questions.

They scared him to death.

CJ was fantastic.

Over and over Gina how thought how lucky she'd been to have a little boy who demanded so little. CJ lived in his own small world, where his imagination ran riot. His requirements from his mother were for security and for hugs and for the basic necessities of life, but as long as those were provided whenever required, he was prepared to accept the assorted childminders he'd met in his short life. He even welcomed them as a wider audience for his incredible stories.

Now, as the helicopter landed at Crocodile Creek and the baby was wheeled into the hospital, as the emergency team sprang into action, Cal motioned to one of the nurses to take care of him.

'Gina's a doctor,' he said briefly—brusquely. 'She's a cardiologist, right when we need one most. We need her help with the baby. Grace, can you find someone to take care of Gina's little boy?'

'Sure.' Grace, a young nurse with a wide smile, held out

her hand to CJ and beamed a welcome. 'I hear you guys have been out at the rodeo. Did you see many horses?'

'I saw lots of horses,' CJ told her, ready to be friendly.

'Will you tell me about them while we find you some juice and some cake? Come to the kitchen. Mrs Grubb is making chocolate cake and she loves hearing about horses. If we're lucky, I think there might even be an icing bowl to lick.'

CJ was sold. He cast an enquiring glance at his mother for approval, then tucked his hand into Grace's and disappeared cakewards.

'He's a great kid,' Mike said as the paramedic wheeled the trolley through into Paediatrics, and Gina gave him a glance that she hoped was grateful.

She looked back at Cal. There was no gratitude there. His face was set and stern.

Maybe she should have phoned him four years ago.

Or not.

Maybe she shouldn't be here now.

If she hadn't been here now, this baby would be dead.

'We need an echocardiogram,' Cal said. He hadn't paused as they moved through the hospital. He was intent only on the baby. Or he acted as if he was intent only on the baby.

'You said you don't have a cardiologist? No one with cardiology training?'

'No.'

'A paediatrician?'

'Hamish is on leave. We're trying to contact him now.'

'We're dead short of doctors,' Mike said, and smiled, but then his smile faded a little. 'There's been a couple of...disasters. Just lucky you're here, huh?'

'I guess,' she said dubiously, and cast an uncertain look at Cal. His face said there was no luck about it.

But she couldn't look at his face. She needed to focus. This baby needed skills that she possessed.

* * *

He certainly did.

When the results of the echocardiograph were in front of her she felt her heart sink. Any thoughts she had of flying out of this place tonight were completely gone.

'It's pulmonary stenosis.'

With the stethoscope she'd been able to hear the characteristic heart murmur at the left upper chest. That and the fast heart rate had made her fairly sure what was causing the cyanosis. And now... Her fears were confirmed. There was a huge pressure difference between the right ventricle and the pulmonary artery. Blood flowing in one direction and unable to escape fast enough in the other. Recipe for catastrophe.

'We can't risk transfer to Brisbane,' Cal said slowly—reluctantly. 'We'll lose him.'

'What's happening?' Mike asked. He'd come in and watched as they worked, but he'd been on the sidelines. Another nurse was there now—a woman in her thirties who'd been introduced as Jill Shaw, the director of nursing. Jill was wheeling the baby back under the nursery lights, with instructions to keep warming, keep monitoring breathing, while the three of them were left staring at the results.

'We operate,' Gina said, staring down at her fingers as if there were some sort of easy answer to be read there. There wasn't. They really needed a paediatric cardiologist, but the nearest available would be in Brisbane and to transfer the baby...

They would have had to if she hadn't been here. They'd have been forced to. Cal was an excellent general surgeon, she thought, and his additional physician training made him a wonderful all-rounder in this place where multi-skills were vital. She knew that. Cal's skills were one of the things that had attracted her to him in the first place.

But the operation for pulmonary stenosis on such a tiny child...

The heart valve they'd be working on—the pulmonary

valve—was thin, even in adults. Composed of three coverlets, like leaflets, it opened in the direction of the blood flow. With pulmonary stenosis those leaflets were blocked or malformed in some way. In the baby's case it was a major blockage. His heart was being forced to work far too hard to force blood through.

What she needed to do was to perform a balloon pulmonary valvuloplasty—a tricky manoeuvre even in adults—forcing the valve to open. With babies this size…

She'd normally advise waiting, she thought bleakly. She'd normally advise keeping him on oxygen. She'd try and get him fitter, older. She'd operate at a few weeks.

To operate on such a newborn…

But this was no minor blockage.

'Do you have the equipment?' she asked. 'I'd need to monitor catheters by fluoroscopy.'

'I'd imagine we have all you need,' Cal told her. 'Simon, the cardiologist who's just left, had the place well set up for heart surgery.'

Gina nodded. She'd worked with this service before, and she'd expected this answer.

Many of the population around Crocodile Creek would be indigenous Australians, and she knew from experience how reluctant they were to leave their people. For a tribal elder to come to Crocodile Creek for an operation would be hugely stressful, but here at least here they could still be surrounded by their own. To be flown to Brisbane, where there was no one of their tribe and no one spoke their language, was often tantamount to killing them. The cultural shock was simply too great for them to handle.

That would be part of the reason Crocodile Creek would be set up so well, she knew. This base would do surgery which would normally only be done in the big teaching hospitals.

Death rates would be higher because of it, but the population would accept it. The doctors involved had to accept it.

But this doctor in particular didn't have to like it.

'So we have no paediatrician and no cardiologist.'

'We're not normally this short-staffed,' Cal told her. 'We've had a couple of dramas.'

He sounded defensive, she thought. Good. It stopped her thinking about all sorts of things she should be defensive about.

'Do you have an obstetrician?'

'Georgie's mother died last week. She's flown down to Sydney with her little boy, and we don't want to pull her back unless we have to. She had back-up—Kirsty was an obs and gynae registrar—but there was a bit of a dust-up and Kirsty and Simon left in a hurry. Emotional stuff.'

'Emotional stuff?' she demanded, astonished, and he looked even more discomfited.

'Um, yeah. We don't need to go there.'

Of course not. When had he ever?

But she had a baby to take care of. Cal's emotional entanglement, or lack of it, had to wait.

Mike was waiting for her to make a decision. He was looking interested—as interested in the chemistry between them as he was in the baby—and that made her flush. She remembered how intimate working in this sort of environment could be. She even remembered enjoying it, but she didn't relish the questions she saw forming in Mike's eyes now.

'I'll wait for an hour and reassess,' she said, trying to make her voice calm and professional. 'We need to get him fully warmed and make sure the shock of delivery has worn off. Maybe once he's settled we might get better circulation.'

'But probably not,' Cal said.

'No,' she said heavily. 'Probably not.'

'So Gina'll need to stay.' Mike wasn't sure what was going on—his eyes were still asking questions—but he was certainly

prepared to be friendly while he found out. He gave Cal a rueful smile. 'Just lucky we have plenty of room in the doctors'
quarters, eh?'

Cal's face tightened. 'She can't stay in the doctors' quarters.'

'Why not?' Mike was confused.

'I'll stay in town,' Gina said hurriedly, but Mike shook his
head. He was obviously a skilled paramedic, accustomed to
making hard decisions, fast decisions, and he made one now.

'No way. I'm sorry, Gina, but this baby is sick.' He cast a
dubious glance at Cal—as if he thought Cal might just be los-
ing his mind. 'We all know this baby's high risk. It seems to
me that we need our cardiologist on hand, right here. Wouldn't
you say, Cal?'

'Of course.' The words were tight and blunt. Cal turned
away to pack equipment and Mike shook his head at his
friend. He was obviously still confused.

'Cal's being a bore,' he told Gina, with another dubious
glance at his friend. 'He's tired. Too much work. But there's
plenty of us around here who are gentlemen.' He tried a smile.
'Especially me.' He waited to see if he'd teased a reaction
from Cal, but a reaction wasn't anywhere in sight. 'OK.' He
sighed. 'Let's find your son and find you a bedroom.'

'I'll stay here and monitor the baby,' Cal told them, still
without turning around.

'Of course,' Mike said politely. 'How did I know you were
going to say that?'

'The baby needs monitoring.'

'Of course he does, Dr Jamieson,' Mike agreed. He com-
pressed his lips in disapproval and then he turned to Gina.
'OK. There's obviously just me being a gentleman, but I'm
all yours. Take me or leave me.'

Charles entered the nursery silently, wheeling his chair across
the smooth linoleum until he came to rest against the incuba-

tor under the overhead lights. Cal was gazing down at the baby and, seeing the look of his face, Charles thought, Uh-oh.

'Will we lose him?'

Cal turned and stared, almost unseeingly, down at his friend.

'I don't know. He has a chance.' There was a moment's silence. 'Gina's here.'

'I heard.' Charles hesitated. He'd met Gina before, just the once. He'd been astounded by the change the relationship had wrought on his reserved friend, and when it had gone pear-shaped he'd felt ill. Now Mike had given him a quick update on what was happening, and he was even more concerned. He'd suspected Cal's past would catch up with him sooner or later but, damn, he didn't want him to be presented with it now.

From a selfish point of view they were too many doctors down already. He couldn't afford to have another of his staff in emotional crisis.

'Are you coping?' he asked, and Cal shrugged.

'I'm coping. You've seen the kid?'

'I've seen the little boy, yes.'

'Dammit, Charles, he looks like me.'

'Could you be his father?'

It was a direct question and it jolted Cal. He stared at the question from all sides and there was only one answer.

'Yeah,' he said heavily. 'I could.'

'And that makes you feel—how?'

'How do you suppose it makes me feel?' Cal turned and faced his friend square on. 'If it's true… She got pregnant and left? Went back to the States to her husband?' He closed his eyes. 'Hell, Charles, I don't want to think about it. I can't think. I don't have time. We need to get this baby viable. He needs urgent surgery and we're stuck with Gina to do it. No one else has the skills.'

He stared down into the crib and his mouth twisted. 'We'll

do the best for him, poor little scrap. He's been abandoned, too. People…they play games. They have kids for all sorts of reasons. Who knows what the reason is behind this little one and who knows what the reason is behind the child who's out in Mrs Grubb's kitchen, waiting for his mother to take him home? I can't face any of it. Just… Let's stick to medicine. It's all I know. It's all I want to know.'

There was a moment's silence. Move on, Cal willed Charles, and finally he seemed to decide that was all there was to do.

'Emily will do the anaesthetic,' Charles said mildly, his voice carefully neutral, not giving away any of the anxiety that someone who knew him well could detect behind his eyes. 'She's contacting a paediatric colleague in the city who'll stay on the phone throughout. Do you want to assist, or will I find someone else?'

'Who?' He was the only surgeon, and both of them knew it. But he shrugged. 'It's OK. I want to assist.'

'So you can bear to be in the same room as her?'

'I thought I loved her,' Cal said heavily. 'Once. I was a fool—but sure I can stay in the same room as her. I need to be able to. If that's really my son…' His voice trailed off.

'Well, let's get on with it,' Charles said, and there was still heavy anxiety behind his eyes. 'We need to save this life. For now, Cal, that's all we can think about.'

CHAPTER THREE

SHE was good.

There was no doubting Dr Gina Lopez's skill. Cal could only watch and wonder.

Not that there was much time for wondering. To operate on a child so young, to insert catheters into such a tiny heart, putting pressure on the faulty valve—that was something that in an adult heart would be tricky but in this pint-sized scrap of humanity seemed impossible.

Emily, the anaesthetist, was at the limits of her capability as well. This procedure should be done by an anaesthetist specialising in paediatrics, but Emily was all they had. She was sweating as she worked, as she monitored the tiny heartbeat, treading the fine line of not enough anaesthetic, or too much and straining this little body past more than it could bear.

Jill, the director of nursing and their most skilled Theatre nurse, was assisting Emily. She was sweating as well.

It was Cal who assisted Gina.

He watched her fingers every step of the way, trying to figure what she was doing, trying to anticipate so there was no delay between her need for a piece of equipment and the time she had it. He was organising, swabbing, waiting for the pauses in her finger movements to reach forward and clear the way for her. Holding things steady. Watching the monitor when she couldn't, guiding her with his voice, and holding catheters steady when she had to focus on the monitor herself.

Grace, their second nurse, was behind him, and she was anticipating as hard as he was.

There was so much need here. Something about this tiny wrinkled newborn had touched them all.

They needed him to live.

They willed him to live.

All that stood between him and death was Gina.

They were lucky that she was here, Cal thought grimly as he helped her painstakingly introduce her catheters from the groin, monitoring herself every inch of the way. No matter why she'd returned after all these years—she'd been in the right place at the right time and this baby could live because of it.

Maybe.

'He's bleeding too much,' she muttered into the stillness, motioning with her eyes to the catheter entry site. 'There has to be an underlying problem.'

'Haemophilia?' Cal asked, and she shook her head.

'I don't think so. It'd be worse. But it's not right. The cord bled too much and we're having trouble here. I want tests. A clotting profile, please, including full blood examination, bleeding time and factor eight levels. Fast.'

'What are we looking for?'

'I don't have time to think. You think. Something.'

He went back to sorting tubing, his mind moving into overdrive. Sifting the facts. She was right. The bleeding was far more severe than it should be. They were fighting to maintain blood pressure.

Why?

'Von Willebrand's?' he said cautiously.

Was he right? Von Willebrand's was a blood disorder that impeded clotting. Like haemophilia, it was genetically linked, passing from parents down to children. It usually wasn't as life-threatening as haemophilia but it did have to be treated. He watched as Gina frowned even more behind her mask. Her fingers were carefully manoeuvring, she was fully absorbed in what she was doing, but he could see her mind start to sort through the repercussions of his tentative diagnosis.

'You could be right,' she said at last. 'It fits.'

'I'll run tests straight away,' he said. 'There's not a lot more we can do about it now, though. And at least it takes away the risks of clotting.'

'Mmm.'

Silence. The tension was well nigh unbearable. She was measuring the pressures in the right ventricle and the pulmonary artery by placing the catheter tip in each area. It was a tricky procedure in an adult, but in a newborn...

'My face,' Gina muttered, and Jill saw her need and stepped forward to wipe sweat beads from above her eyes.

She was good, Cal thought grimly. Good enough?

The work went on. The child's tiny heart kept beating. Emily was fighting with everything she had. She had a paediatric anaesthetist on the line from the city, and she was working with a headset. Her soft voice asking questions was the only sound as they worked.

Cal had seen this done in adults, but he'd never seen the procedure in one so tiny. As a general surgeon he would never think of doing such a procedure himself. He couldn't, he acknowledged. Somewhere along the line Gina had acquired skills that could only make him wonder.

Gina was working out diameters now, her eyes moving from fingers to monitor, fingers to monitor, and he could almost see her brain doing the complex calculations as she worked out the next step forward.

She was brilliant. An amazing surgeon.

The mother of his son?

'Now the wire,' she said into the stillness, and the sound of her voice almost made him start.

Back to silence.

The balloon valvuloplasty catheter was threaded over the wire, painstakingly positioned so its centre was just at the valve. That was the hard part.

Now came the hardest.

Please…

'Let's try,' Gina said into a silence that was close to unbearable. 'I think…'

The balloon was inflated, showing on the monitor under fluoroscopy, with Gina watching that it remained centred all the time. The balloon had been manoeuvred right to the valve. Now it was stretching the valve, much as a shoe was stretched by a cobbler, hoping that once the stretching was done the valve would self-correct. The pressures would equalise.

If it didn't happen, then the build-up of pressure could mean instant heart failure—instant death.

This was no time for panic. The procedure called for infinite patience.

The balloon was inflated once. Twice. Three times the valve was stretched.

'Enough,' Gina said, and Cal heard exhaustion in her voice.

But she couldn't stop now. She had to check the pressures again. If the pressures weren't equalised the whole thing would have to be repeated, using balloons of different lengths and diameters, and this tiny heart was under so much strain anyway…

The catheters were reinserted, once more measuring the pressures in the right ventricle and the pulmonary artery.

Please.

The figures…

'Hey,' Jill said in a tiny tremulous voice that didn't sound the least bit like the efficient director of nursing they all knew—and, if truth be told, they often feared. 'We have lift-off. Isn't that right, Houston?'

'I… Maybe,' Gina said. She glanced up at her anaesthetist. 'What do you think?'

'I think maybe you've done it,' Emily said in a voice that was none too steady. 'Oh, Gina, that was fantastic.'

'Fantastic? It's a miracle,' Gina whispered. 'If we have indeed won. He's not out of the woods yet.'

He wasn't. They all knew that. To operate on such a tiny baby was asking for post-op complications. Indeed, there might well be complications already. He'd stopped breathing that afternoon. He'd had a birth in circumstances that were appalling. And now maybe he was facing a new threat. Von Willebrand's?

For him to pull through…

'He'll make it,' Cal said, and he wasn't sure why he knew or how he knew, it was just definite, absolute knowledge. 'I know he will. You've done it, Gina.'

'Thank God for that, then,' she whispered. 'I'm not as sure as you as to the outcome here, but he has every chance. Maybe…maybe for once in this country I've done something right.'

Three hundred miles away the girl lay beneath her bedcovers and shivered. It was hot out here—so hot—and for her family to afford air-conditioning was unthinkable. But despite the heat, she couldn't stop shivering.

Her baby…

Dead.

'Sweetheart?' It was her mother, knocking on her door for what must be the sixth time since they'd got home from the rodeo. 'Are you OK?'

She sounded worried. That was a laugh. When had her mother ever worried about her?

'Go away.'

'What's wrong?'

'I've got my period. I feel sick. Go away.'

Her mother hesitated and Megan could hear the fear in her voice. 'You're not well enough to feed the poddy calves, then?'

'No. Go away.'

'But your father...'

She roused herself—or she tried to—but the tiredness washing over her body was overwhelming.

'I know Dad's sick,' she whispered, loudly enough for her mother to hear through the battered farmhouse door. 'I know you've got too much to do to manage. But, Mum, I can't. I just can't. For tonight you'll just have to manage without me.'

When she'd done all she could do, Gina stepped away from the table. Her face said it all. Her eyes were drained, her expression slack with exhaustion. She'd called on every resource she had, and then some.

'Can I leave it to you now?' she asked, unsteadily into the stillness. 'I'll be outside. Call me on the PA if you need me. I won't go away. But I need...some air.'

'You deserve some air,' Emily said warmly. 'You even deserve something a bit stronger, like a stiff drink or a cigar. Off you go, Dr Lopez. Cal and I will take it from here. But thank God you were here.'

'Thank you,' Gina whispered, and with a last, uncertain glance down at the table she started to move away.

Then she paused. Her finger dropped for a fleeting moment to trace the tiny cheekbone, to just touch...

'Fight, little one,' she whispered. 'Fight.'

And then she was gone.

'That's one amazing doctor,' Emily said as she left, and Cal could only agree.

'Yeah.'

'Charles said you knew her five years back.' Em was still concentrating but she had room to cast a curious glance at her friend. 'He's saying she's your lady-rat.'

'Leave it, Em.' Dammit, he couldn't think of what else to say. And it was none of her business.

Since when did privacy considerations ever stop anyone in this place sticking their nose in anyone else's business? It certainly didn't stop Em now.

'Charles says there's a little boy.'

'Leave it, Emily,' Cal snapped again—harder—and Emily had the temerity to grin.

'Yes, sir.'

'Is he yours?' Grace asked from behind them, and Cal groaned.

'Look, this is my business.'

'Hey, we're your housemates,' Emily told him. 'And Mike says there's something really funny going on. He's laying odds on this being your son—but no one's taking bets until we've seen him. So tell us, Cal. Save us our betting money. Is it true?'

They were still working, but the atmosphere in the room had lightened by about a thousand per cent. Something about a tiny heartbeat that was steady and growing stronger by the minute was making even such a serious subject sound frivolous.

'You might as well tell us. You know we share all your dearest concerns,' Emily told him, and Grace choked.

'That's another way of saying we have a right to stick our nose into whatever we like.'

'I don't know how you do it, Cal.' For once Jill was also smiling, the nursing director's tight personality unbending a little in the face of this shared triumph. 'Having all your concerns shared. Ten medicos living in the same house…'

'Eight as of Tuesday,' Grace reminded her, and Emily winced.

'Thanks very much.'

'He was a creep, Em, and you know it,' Grace retorted. 'I refuse to concede that you can possibly mourn the guy.'

'I'll mourn anyone I like.'

'Why don't you have an affair with Cal?'

'Cal's got an affair,' Emily retorted. 'As of now.' She managed a smile. 'Actually, an affair and a bit. A bit about three feet high. So concentrate on Cal's love life. Leave mine alone.'

'OK,' Grace said obligingly. 'If you insist. And Cal's affair is fascinating. A woman and a son arriving out of nowhere, when we all thought he was a fusty old bachelor...'

'Thanks a lot,' Cal managed, and even Jill chuckled.

'But here he is, with a son...'

'Is he really your son?' Jill asked, wondering, and Cal groaned.

'Jill, at least you can keep out of what's not your business.'

'We love you, Cal,' Emily said solidly. 'Get used to it.'

'I don't think I ever will.'

'It's called living,' Em told him, and she turned from the monitor to look down at her little patient. 'Something this little man is about to do. Oh, well done, us. Now all we need to do is find you a mummy and a daddy.'

'And find out whether Cal's a daddy, too,' Grace said mischievously.

'Enough.' Jill had been jolted out of clinical efficiency but her flashes of humour never lasted long. There was levity in her operating Theatre and levity was to be squashed. 'Back to work.'

'Yes, ma'am,' they said in unison.

Where was Gina? All Cal wanted to do was to find her, and he couldn't.

There were myriad things to do before he was finished. Blood tests to order. Harry Blake to be contacted—the police sergeant who'd be in charge of trying to find the mother. A mass of paperwork that had to be done—now. 'Because this case will hit the national press unless I'm mistaken, and I want everything done right,' Charles had growled.

Charles himself wheeled into Theatre at the end and stared down at the little one in concern.

'Do we have any clue who the mother could be?'

'None at all,' Cal told him. 'We're sifting through obs and gynae records now, looking at who's pregnant in the area.'

'One of our tribal people? Maybe some kid who's got herself pregnant out of tribal boundaries?'

'Take a longer look, Charles. I'm guessing this baby's all white. Mum and Dad both.'

'Surely we have pregnancy records.'

'Unless it was someone who's itinerant. Someone who came for the day.'

They stared at the baby for a moment longer, searching for answers.

There were none.

'I guess we have to leave that to Harry,' Charles said reluctantly, spinning his chair in a one-eighty-degree turn and shrugging as he talked of handing things over to the police. 'I hate not knowing as much as you do. Harry's just rung in to say they're searching the area and I'll tell him to increase the manpower. To think there's a kid out there who's only hours from giving birth…'

'And she may be suffering from von Willebrand's disease,' Cal told him, outlining his concerns.

Charles's face stilled. 'So she's likely to be bleeding. She could be in huge trouble.

'Von Willebrand's could be inherited from the father. If indeed I'm right. It's only that the baby's bleeding too much, too fast. I'm only guessing the diagnosis here.'

'Then keep on guessing,' Charles said heavily, 'Guess as much as you can and as fast as you can. I want her found.'

'Right.' Cal hesitated. 'Do we move him down to Bris-bane?'

'Not yet,' Charles said heavily. 'I'm calling in Hamish from leave. If the mother's found I want this little one right here, where she has the best chance of bonding with him—or making any decision she needs to make. It's a risk, but if I can persuade Gina to stay then it's a risk I'm prepared to take.'

Cal nodded. Hamish, Crocodile Creek's paediatrician, was out game fishing but it should be possible to call him back. If this base had both a paediatrician and a cardiologist, then it was reasonable to leave this little one here. Good, even.

But would Gina stay?'

'Charles, I also need to find Gina.'

'Sure you do, Charles agreed. 'Get these tests organised, talk to Harry and then go find her. She's over at the house, out on the veranda.'

Of course. Charles knew where everyone was, all the time.

'I'll go, then.'

'You do that.'

She was alone.

Cal walked out the back door of the doctors' residence and Gina was sitting on the back step, staring out over the sea.

The old hospital used now as doctors' quarters and the new state-of-the-art Remote Rescue base were built on a bluff overlooking Crocodile Cove—a wide, sandy beach with gentle waves washing in and out of the gently sloping shallows. In the foreground lay the Agnes Wetherby Memorial Garden. The garden was fantastic—a mass of tropical plants such as the delicately perfumed orchids, creamy, heady frangipani, crotons with their vividly coloured leaves, and more. A wide natural rockpool lay off centre surrounded by giant ferns, and from the veranda Cal could hear the soft croak of tree frogs enjoying its lush dampness.

Beyond the garden was the rock-strewn slope leading down to the beach—thick grassland dotted with moonflowers, their fat leaves looking just like butterfly wings. The sunlight glinted through the garden, the soft wind shifting the dappled shade. It was beautiful.

Gina was beautiful.

He'd thought that the first time he'd seen her, and nothing had changed. Not a thing.

She wasn't dressed to attract. She never had. Now, in faded jeans, a stained T-shirt that was truly horrible, battered sneakers…

Yep, she was beautiful.

He walked over, sat down beside her and stared out over the sea, as if trying to see what she was seeing. This was a beautiful setting.

'Sorry.' She winced and moved sideways. 'It's been too big a day. The rodeo. The baby. Surgery. I…I need to find a shower.'

'You definitely need to find a shower,' he told her. 'But it was blood gained in a battle worth fighting. Well done.'

'Thanks.'

They stared some more at the sea. Trying to figure out where to start. Where was he supposed to start? Surely it was up to her. To do this to him…

She kept her silence. Seemingly it was up to him.

'Would you like to tell me,' he said finally into the still-ness, 'just what is going on?'

'We may just have saved a baby.'

'Gina…'

'Sorry.'

'Is CJ…mine?'

She glanced at him then—and then looked away as if she couldn't bear to see him. Which was maybe exactly how he'd expect her to feel.

'Yes,' she whispered.

More silence.

'Hell,' he said at last, and she nodded as if that was no more than she'd expected.

'I guess it is.'

There was anger building now, an anger so overwhelming it was all he could do to stay still, not to stand up and crash his fist into the veranda pole, not to yell...

Yelling would achieve nothing. He had to stay calm.

'So.' He stared out to sea some more, not looking at her, not wanting to look at her. 'So I got used.'

'I— What do you mean?'

'You and your husband used me as a sperm donor.'

'Cal, it wasn't like that.' She turned to him, her face puckering in distress. 'It wasn't. I need to tell you...'

'That's what it seems like to me,' he said savagely. 'You come out here, you say you love me, you con me into taking you to bed—'

Her breath drew in, shocked, stunned. 'Cal, I never did. I wouldn't.'

'And then you leave. You just leave.' His anger was clearly apparent in his voice and there was no way he could disguise it. 'You just disappear.'

'I wrote.'

'Yeah, and told me that your husband—who I'd thought was no longer in the picture—needed you and you were going back to him. You wouldn't answer questions. Nothing. And when I tried to phone you—when I eventually found you through your hospital—you wouldn't talk to me.'

'I couldn't answer questions,' she told him. 'I just couldn't.' Her voice trailed away. 'I couldn't bear to.'

'You couldn't bear to tell me you'd used me?'

'Please, don't, Cal,' she whispered. 'It wasn't like that. You know it wasn't. What we had was amazing.'

'Yeah, it was, wasn't it?' he said heavily into the stillness. 'Mind-blowing. It was sex. Was that all it was? Great sex, Gina, followed by pregnancy, and then back to your husband so you can play happy families?'

'You're not going to let me explain?'

'Mom?' The voice came from behind them. CJ. The little boy stood in the doorway behind the screen door, looking from his mother to Cal and back again. 'Mrs Grubb said you've finished saving the baby. Have you?'

'Yes, we have, CJ,' she told him, visibly gathering her wits. As he came through the door she held out a hand to tug him close. Then she gestured to Cal, took a deep breath and performed introductions. 'CJ, this is Cal. CJ, this is the very special Australian friend I've been telling you for about all these years. The man I hoped we'd get to visit while we were over here.'

'The man with my name?' CJ asked, and Gina nodded.

'That's right.'

'Hi.' CJ put out his hand, man to man. 'I'm Callum James Michelton. I'm very pleased to meet you.'

Callum James.

CJ.

Cal swallowed. His hand was still being gripped so he shook the child's hand with due solemnity and then released it.

'My mom says you're the best doctor in the world,' CJ told him. 'And she says you can juggle better than anyone she knows.'

It was hard, getting his voice to work. Cal swallowed again and tried harder. 'Your mom told you that?'

'She told me lots about you. She says you're terrific.' CJ eyed Cal cautiously, as if he was prepared to give his mother the benefit of the doubt for a while but Cal just might have to prove himself. 'You've got the same colour hair as I have.'

'Is it the same colour as your dad's?' Stupid question.

Stupid, stupid question, and he felt Gina flinch, but he'd asked it and now he had to wait for an answer.

'My dad's dead,' CJ told him. 'He was in a wheelchair and he had black hair and a big scar down the side of his face.' He sighed. 'My dad watched TV with me and he read me stories but then he got so sick that he died. I miss him a lot and a lot.'

'I… I see.'

He didn't see. There were so many unanswered questions.

'Are we talking about Paul here?' he asked—feeling his way—and Gina nodded.

'That's right. Paul.'

'So when you said your marriage was over…'

'CJ, do you think you could bring me out a glass of water?' Gina asked, and there was a note of desperation in her voice. 'Would Mrs Grubb give you one for me?'

'Sure,' CJ told her. 'We've made choc-chip cookies with twice the number of choc chips in the recipe 'cos Mrs Grubb let me tip and I spilt them. They're warm.' He turned to Cal. 'Would you like one, sir?'

'Yes, please,' Cal managed. 'Um…call me Cal.'

'Yes, sir. I mean Cal. I'll be an aeroplane. I haven't been an aeroplane all day.' He was off, zooming along the veranda, arms outstretched.

'CJ,' his mother called, and he stopped in mid-flight.

'Yeah?'

'This is a hospital and some sick patients might be going to sleep. Do you think you could be a silent glider instead of an aeroplane?'

'Sure, I can.' CJ put his lips firmly together. 'Shh,' he ordered himself, 'If you make one loud noise up here, you'll scare the eagles.'

And off he glided, kitchenwards.

Cal was left staring after him.

'Great kid,' he said at last—cautiously—and Gina nodded.

'Yeah. He takes after his daddy.'

'Paul…'

'You.'

He sighed. The anger had gone now. All that was left was an ineffable weariness. A knowledge that somehow he'd been used and somehow this child had been born and there'd been four years of a child growing in his image that he'd known nothing about.

'Tell me,' he said.

She shrugged. 'In a nutshell?'

'Take your time.' His voice was heavy. He hardly wanted to know himself. If she didn't want to tell him…

But it seemed she did.

'Some of it you know,' she said, her voice distant now, as if repeating a learned-by-heart story. 'I told you the bare facts when we first met. That I'd been married and that I was separated.'

'But—'

'Just let me tell it, Cal,' she whispered, and he stared at her for a long minute, and then nodded.

'I'm listening.'

'Big of you.'

'Gina…'

'I married Paul when I was eighteen,' she told him, and there was a blankness about her voice now that hadn't been there before. 'He was the boy next door, the kid I'd grown up with. We decided to marry when we were twelve. We went through med school together, we were best of friends—and then suddenly he just seemed to fall apart. There'd been huge pressure on him from his parents to become a doctor. To marry. To be successful in their eyes. Maybe I was stupid for not seeing how much pressure he was under.'

'You weren't sympathetic toward him when you were here,' he said, and she nodded.

'No. I was young and I was hurt. We'd made it as doctors, we had the world at our feet and suddenly he didn't want any part of our life together. He wanted to find himself, he said, and off he went. And to be honest it wasn't until I decided to come here…until I met you…that I realised that he was right. We'd been kids, playing at being grown-ups. We'd married for the wrong reasons.'

'So?' He wasn't going to get sucked into the emotional bit here, he thought. He couldn't afford to.

'So then I fell for you,' she said softly. 'And I got pregnant.'

He closed his eyes, trying to think back to all that time ago. But it didn't make sense. He'd never been stupid. He of all people knew the risks. 'How can you have got pregnant? We took precautions.'

'Are you saying I'm lying?' Anger flashed out then, bordering on fury. 'Do you think I planned the pregnancy?'

'I don't know what to think.'

'Well, think what you like,' she snapped. 'But I didn't plan it. I was on the Pill. I knew how much you didn't want children, and I was hardly in a position to want them either. So we were careful. But I guess there's truth in the saying that the only sure contraceptive is two brick walls with air space between. Whatever we used didn't work. Anyway, I couldn't believe it. I discovered I was pregnant when you were upcountry on a medical evacuation flight. You were gone. I was down in Townsville, staring at a positive pregnancy test. Thinking I couldn't tell you. I couldn't.'

His eyes opened at that and he met her look head on. Challenging. 'Why the hell not?'

'What would you have said?' she whispered. 'Be honest, Cal. How would you have reacted?'

'How do I know?'

'Well, I know,' she said drearily. 'You'd said it over and over to me. You didn't want family. Your family life was the pits. You never wanted commitment. Sure, what we had was special and we both knew it, but it wasn't enough to make you want marriage. Or children. The thought appalled you. You said it over and over. It was like a warning. Love me despite it—and I did. I was willing to accept you on your terms. But then I fell pregnant. I sat there staring at the test strip and I thought, I can't get rid of this baby. Maybe I did my growing up right there. I wanted this baby. I wanted our baby.'

He shook his head, bewildered. 'Gina, if I'd known—'

'You might even have done the honourable thing,' she said heavily. 'I knew that. But honour wasn't what I wanted from you, Cal, and you were capable of offering nothing more.'

'I might have—'

'No.' She shook her head. 'I knew your background, you see, though I heard much of it from others. Not from you.'

'My background has nothing to do with this.'

'It has everything, Cal,' she said heavily. 'If I don't accept it, at least I can understand. Your mother walked out on you when you were still a kid yourself, trapping you into caring for your two little sisters. Your father was a drunk. You had to leave school to support everyone and then, just as your sisters started being independent, your mother reappeared and offered your sisters a home in the States with her new man. But not you. After all you'd done, they left you without a backward glance. Your dad died and you had to regroup and work your butt off to get yourself through medical school. You learned in the hardest way to be independent. Do you think I was going to trap you again?'

'Hell…'

'It was hell,' she whispered. 'For both of us. For different reasons.'

'So you just ran.'

'Strangely, I didn't,' she told him, and her chin jutted, just a little. Finding her feet again. This part of the story was easier. 'While I was trying to sort some sense out of the mess the phone rang and it was Paul's mother. It was…as if it was meant. It was horrible but it was real. She rang to tell me that Paul had been injured—dreadfully injured—in a motorbike accident in Kathmandu. She was distraught. She couldn't go herself. Could I go? she asked. She pleaded. There was no one else. I had medical training and that was what Paul desperately needed. Family and western medicine. So…' She paused and stared blankly out over the sea. 'So I just went.'

He stared at her, still disbelieving. 'Without waiting for me to get back?'

'You were gone for two days. Paul's mother thought he was dying. I had to move fast. As it was, I only just got there in time. I found him in a tiny village outside the capital and he was dreadfully injured. From then on the drama of the situation just took over. Getting him stabilised. He'd smashed his spine, and the convolutions to evacuate him back to the States took weeks. And then…by the time I'd caught my breath, somehow I was three months pregnant and I was back to being Paul's wife again.'

'That was what your note said,' he said heavily, remembering. 'That Paul had been injured and you were still his wife and you were staying with him. That your marriage had resumed.'

'I didn't lie.'

'No,' he said. 'I guess you didn't.'

There was a long silence then. There wasn't tension here. It was as if the world had somehow paused and was regrouping.

But finally the questions started again.

'How badly was Paul hurt?'

That was easy. 'Break at C1/2. Complete quadriplegia. No function below the neck and barely speech,' she told him. 'No unaided respiration. The guy he crashed into had basic medical training so they were able to establish an air supply. Maybe that was a good thing. Sometimes I don't know. But

Paul had almost five years of life before the infections became too frequent and his body shut down.'

'You don't think,' Cal said carefully into the stillness, 'that it might have been fair to tell me this?'

'What? That I still loved you but I'd decided I needed to stay with Paul? How could I tell you that? It wasn't even fair. If I had to stay with Paul, what was the use of telling you I loved you? Besides,' she said softly into the stillness, 'you knew that I loved you. I'd told you that over and over. But you'd never said it back to me. Not once, Cal. Not ever.'

'I…' He paused and she shrugged, moving on.

'It doesn't matter,' she told him. 'Not now. And it couldn't matter then. Cal, Paul had no one except his elderly mother who was incapacitated herself. He needed me so much. And when CJ was born…'

'Yeah, that's what I can't understand,' he snapped. 'How he accepted another man's son.'

'CJ gave him pleasure,' she told him. 'Huge pleasure. You know, when Paul learned I was pregnant he didn't even ask who the father was. I said I'd had a love affair that hadn't worked out and he didn't want to know more. But the pregnancy itself made him…joyful. It was as if something good had come from the mess he'd created. For the few years left of his life, CJ was the centre of Paul's life. And Paul had been my friend for ever. I couldn't take that away from him.'

'You took it away from me.'

Her eyes flashed at that. 'You didn't want it,' she said, steadily now, as if she was on ground she was sure of. 'When I found out that I was pregnant I was appalled. I knew you didn't want a child. I knew you didn't want a family. Am I right, Cal?'

Was she right?

He stared at her and he couldn't answer.

Of course he didn't want kids. He never had. Damn, with

his family, how could he? Kids were a disaster. Commitment was a disaster.

'Maybe,' he said—grudgingly—and she winced and hauled herself to her feet.

'There you go, then. So I kept my son where at least someone wanted him. Paul was his daddy, and Paul loved him more than life itself.'

'And you,' he said softly. 'Did you love Paul?'

'Don't be stupid, Cal,' she said heavily. 'To ask a question like that... Don't be so daft.'

He stared at her, wondering where to go from here. Where...

'Here are the cookies! I have cookies.' There was a triumphant stage whisper from behind them. The glider was flying cautiously back through the screen door, bearing two glasses of water and four choc-chip cookies, all balanced precariously on a plastic tray.

'Bruce is in the kitchen,' CJ told them in satisfaction, handing over his burden with care. 'He says he's really pleased to see us and can he take us out to dinner?'

'Bruce?' He was almost grateful for the interruption, Cal decided. For something else to focus on. Emotions were threatening to overwhelm him.

'It'll be Bruce Hammond,' Gina told him. 'We met Bruce while we were staying here. He took us on a crocodile hunt but we didn't find any.'

'We did,' CJ retorted. 'It was only the grown-ups who said it was a log.'

'You were staying here?' Cal asked, dazed. How could they have been staying here? This wasn't making sense.

'We've been staying at the Athina Hotel for the last three days,' she told him. 'Just near here. When Paul died, I thought...well, I thought that maybe you had the right to know about CJ. So we came to see you. But on the night we arrived you were out here on the veranda with—Emily, isn't it? I thought…' Her voice trailed off. 'It just seemed like such an imposition after all these years.'

'It *is* an imposition,' he muttered, and his voice was almost savage.

She nodded, as if she'd expected nothing less. 'So I decided to go again.'

'Without seeing me?'

'You didn't want this, Cal,' she told him, lifting her chin again and meeting his look full on. 'I always knew what you thought of family. Anyway, Bruce was nice to us. He wanted us to go out with him again and try to find more crocodiles, but I said we were leaving town. I guess he's heard we're back.' She took a deep breath, moving on, and glanced at her watch. 'I guess we could go out for a quick dinner with Bruce.'

'There's dinner here,' Cal growled. 'And you might be needed for the baby.'

'I won't go far,' she said, steadily, as if she was fighting to keep control on her temper. 'I imagine there's a cellphone I can borrow.'

'Bruce says he knows where crocodiles really love to be,' CJ told her, and she managed a smile.

'No crocodiles tonight, CJ. I think we've had enough adventure. But Bruce will tell you about them.' She turned again to Cal. 'Cal, I'm sorry to land this on you. I never meant to. I never wanted… But, anyway, now you know. I won't be an imposition. I won't make any demands. We'll stay until the baby doesn't need us any more. We certainly won't interfere with what's between you and Emily, and then we'll go.'

She hesitated, and then, as if determined to do something that she wasn't sure would be welcomed, she suddenly leaned forward. She kissed him lightly, a feather kiss, fleetingly on the lips, and then she backed off. Fast.

'I've owed you that for a long time,' she whispered. 'Regardless of what's been between us in the past. This is what I need to say. Thank you for my son, Cal. CJ's been the only thing that's stood between me and madness for the past few years. For both Paul and me. I love CJ so much and Paul did, too. I hope you've found that loving with Emily. Believe me, I'm not here to interfere. If you've found your true home… I won't put that in jeopardy for anything.'

And before he could reply—before he could even think about replying—she'd risen and taken CJ's hand, and turned and walked inside.

Leaving him staring after her. With two glasses of water and four truly excellent choc-chip cookies.

By the time Cal left the veranda it was all over the hospital. Cal had a son. Cal's son and Cal's ex-girlfriend had gone out to dinner with the local crocodile hunter. Everyone wanted to know more.

Cal tried for a little privacy at dinner by glowering at everyone who asked questions—but that created even more questions.

At least Gina wasn't there. She'd spent time with Emily, stabilising the baby. Then she and CJ had disappeared with Bruce, and watching them go had made Cal glower even more. Em had found her a cellphone. Bruce promised to have her back here in minutes if was needed.

But he still glowered. His friends prodded and laughed and then finally they backed off, realising that information wasn't going to be forthcoming. But he knew the questions were still there.

He had unanswered questions himself.

After dinner he headed back to the veranda, looking for some peace. He had medico-legal paperwork to do but it held no attraction. It was eight o'clock and then eight-thirty. They should be back, he thought, and tried not to look up every time a car approached.

Finally he gave up car-watching and headed next door to

the hospital. Surely there was something that needed doing. Something that could distract him. Where was work when you needed it most? These last few days had been crazy.

Now there was nothing. Even the baby didn't need him. They'd decided to keep a doctor within arm's reach and Em was taking first shift.

But still he visited the nursery. This little one was so small. Things could go either way here, Cal thought, jolted out of his preoccupation with the personal by the sight of their tiny patient. The baby was hooked to tubes everywhere. He was the fragile centre of a huge spiderweb of technology and all of it might not be enough to save him.

They'd discussed again the idea of sending for the neonatal evacuation team to take him to a specialist facility, but Em wasn't happy with the idea. Gina had concurred and the paediatrician in Brisbane had agreed. There was nothing a specialist facility could do that wasn't being done here, and the flight itself would be a risk.

As Cal entered the nursery Em looked up from checking the oxygen level and managed a faint smile.

'Hi.'

'Hi, yourself. How's he doing?'

'Holding on. It's all we can hope for. We're calling him Lucky, because he's lucky to be alive.' She hesitated. 'And maybe because he needs still more luck.'

Cal grimaced. He reached in to touch the soft skin of the baby's tiny face and felt his gut twist in sympathy for this fragile little life.

'You live, Lucky,' he told him gruffly.

He had to.

'Is there any news of the mother?' Em asked.

'There's a search party scouring the bushland around the rodeo grounds, but there's nothing. The current thinking is that whoever it was left with the crowd.'

She flicked a glance up at him. 'And left her son.'

'She probably thought he was dead. He was so flat… He may well have appeared dead to someone who had no med training. Someone who was distressed and desperately ill herself.'

She nodded bleakly and then turned her attention back to the baby. 'He almost was dead,' she whispered. 'He came so close. Oh, Lucky. If not for Gina. And now… Another little boy.'

'Em…' He knew where she was going. The way he said her name was a growl, meant to deflect her, but it didn't work.

'Did you know you had a child?'

'No. Em, I—'

'I can't believe you have a son,' she told him, and Cal hesitated. And then he shrugged. This was Emily. His friend. He knew from long experience it was no use to try and deflect her, so why not vent a little spleen? He surely had spleen to be vented.

'If you can't believe it, imagine how I feel!' he demanded, but he didn't get the reaction he wanted. He expected indignation on his behalf—that was what he wanted. Even sympathy. Instead, Emily had the temerity to smile.

'Yep, I can see how it might leave you flabbergasted. A child out of left field. Does she want child support?'

'No!'

'Then why has she come?'

'She just thought I had the right to know.'

'After all these years? Why not sooner?'

'She's been married,' Cal told her. 'She was married when I knew her. She got pregnant and went back to her husband.'

'Whew.' Em whistled, then lifted the drug sheet beside the crib and studied it. Giving him a bit of personal space. 'That's heavy stuff,' she commented. 'Did you know she was married?'

'Yes, but I thought it was over.'

'But it wasn't.'

'Apparently not.'

'So what's happened now to make things different? Marriage break up?'

'Her husband's dead.'

'Dead?'

'Quadriplegia. Complications.'

She winced. 'Oh, Cal, that's really tough.'

Tough? He didn't want to think about tough, he thought bitterly. He didn't want to think about what Gina must have gone through over the last few years.

He didn't want to think about Gina.

'Did she use you to get pregnant?' Em asked, adjusting the drip stand so she could get a clearer view of the baby's tiny face. 'Because her husband was a quad?'

'No!' It was his turn to wince. OK, that was what *he'd* thought initially, but somehow…that someone else should think that of Gina was unbearable. 'He was injured just after she discovered she was pregnant.'

'Ouch.' She flicked another glance up at him and then looked away. 'So that's why the loyalty. That's why she went back to him.'

'Em, could we leave this?'

She looked at him steadily then, her intelligent eyes turning thoughtful. 'Maybe we can and maybe we can't. So now her husband's dead and she comes back—'

'Em…'

'It puts a different complexion on things,' she said, unperturbed. 'I always wondered how the guy would feel in such a situation. To be unexpectedly a full-fledged dad. And for Gina to front you now… It'd be so hard. But maybe she's right.' She cocked her head to one side, considering. 'I wonder. Even if you'd done this via a sperm bank, maybe there's a moral obligation to tell you that your sperm's successful? That's there's a kid out there in your image?'

'He wasn't the result of any sperm bank. Em, we need to write up these notes.'

'Yeah, Charles told me it was a really hot affair.' Em grinned, refusing to be deflected. 'Not a sperm bank at all. This is the one that gossip says broke your heart. Charles said she really cracked your armour and it's the only time in your life it's ever been cracked. Well, now.'

'Em…'

'Hey, but she's here and you don't have an excuse to be heartbroken any more.' Em even looked cheerful. 'You've been using the excuse that you loved and lost for five long years. You've been using it to keep the world and commitment at bay. Now you can take up where you left off. And she's not married. You know, I'll bet that was one of the things that attracted you to her in the first place. I can see letting yourself fall for a divorcée with as jaded a view of commitment as you have. But now… I wonder what you'll decide to do now?'

'What the—?'

'She's been an excuse, hasn't she, Cal?' Em said softly, boring right to the heart of the matter. There was something about this time, this place—the dim light of the nursery with only this one tiny baby between them—that made a conversation like this seem possible. Or less impossible. 'All these years, you've been telling yourself that you haven't got involved with anyone because Gina broke your heart. You've been letting us all think you still love Gina.'

'I don't,' he snapped. But… Did he?

'Then why haven't you gone out with other women?'

'I have. Look, can we leave this?'

'Of course,' she agreed. 'But as for going out with other women… Sure you do, until they get the first idea that they might be able to expect some emotional return. Then you drop them like hot coals. And if you think the rest of the staff in the house will leave it, you're very much mistaken. Are you taking over here at nine?'

'Nine till twelve. Yes.'

'There you go, then.' She turned back to her little patient. 'We'll just have to keep you alive until then, won't we, Lucky?' Her face softened. 'And then it's Dr Cal's turn to keep you alive. Or Dr Gina's, or whoever else is on duty. But we will keep you alive.'

The intensity of her voice shocked him.

'Of course we will,' he told her, and she looked up and met his eyes. Her own eyes welled with tears.

'There's a mother out there who doesn't have a son,' she whispered. 'It's our job to keep our Lucky safe until we find her. But isn't it strange that on this day, when we've found this unknown baby, you've found your own son?' She smiled at him, a wavering smile that said as much about her own fragile emotional state as it did about her uncertainty over the little boy's fate. 'Go on, now, Cal. I have a job to do. And maybe you do, too. See if you can find CJ before you come back on duty. You have years of catching up to do.'

CHAPTER FOUR

THE house was still when Cal returned. Unusually still. Everyone must be out, he decided. Or busy.

Half their luck.

He grabbed a beer but then replaced it. With regret. He could really use a beer, but if he was to go back on duty at nine he had to leave it.

Why was the kitchen empty? And the lounge? Where was everyone? This house was always full of people. He needed people.

He needed people now.

The door swung wide and he turned, but it wasn't the people he wanted. Or maybe it was.

'Hi.' It was Gina. And CJ. His son.

They'd been laughing, he thought. CJ was still smiling broadly and there was a trace of a smile fading from Gina's face. Gina had showered and changed since he'd last seen her. Apparently her luggage was on the coach to Cairns, but someone had lent her jeans and a soft blue and white gingham blouse. She'd brushed her dark curls until they shone and she looked…she looked…

'Did you have a good evening?' he managed, but then he had to think for a minute to figure out what his words meant. Everything seemed disoriented.

Luckily CJ noticed nothing strange. He was more than prepared to chat. 'Bruce took us to Athina's for dinner 'cos he says Mrs Poulos makes the best food in town,' he told him. 'And tomorrow he says he'll take us crocodile hunting again.'

'I'm not sure whether we can go,' Gina told him.

'But we have to go. And he gave me this hat.' This was obviously the highlight of the evening. The little boy was wearing a vast, battered Akubra Cal would have recognised from a mile away.

'Bruce gave you his hat?' Here was another astonishment. Cal knew Bruce well, and he knew the croc hunter lived in this hat.

But apparently no longer.

'He says it's time he got a new one,' CJ said proudly, lifting it off his head to poke his finger through a hole, centre-front. 'I asked him if this was from a bullet and he said it might have been.'

'Bedtime, CJ.' Gina was steering CJ firmly toward the door.

CJ balked, planting his feet. Bracing himself.

'Can Cal read me a story?'

'Cal's busy.'

'He doesn't look busy.'

'CJ…'

'I'll read him a story.'

'You—'

'Have you told CJ anything about me?' He was angry, he decided, sorting through the myriad emotions he was experiencing and choosing the one in the forefront. He hadn't met this kid until now, and CJ—*his* son—was wearing another man's hat.

'I've told CJ that you've been a friend of mine for a long time.' Gina's voice was carefully neutral. 'I guess…if you do want to read to him then it's fine.'

'I do want.'

'Then I'll help him brush his teeth and put on his pjs. Jill's found us some gear to keep us going until I can retrieve my luggage. So… His bedroom in five minutes?'

'Fine.'

Why had he done that? This was a crazy situation. He didn't want to get involved.

He *was* involved.

CJ had beamed up at him from underneath Bruce's hat and…

And he was involved right up to his neck.

It was Gina's turn to sit alone on the veranda.

The big French windows leading to her son's bedroom were wide open. She could hear everything that was going on inside. So she sat, staring out at the moonlit sea, listening to Cal's deep voice reading her son a story.

This was CJ's favourite book, carried everywhere in his backpack, and she must have read it to him a thousand times. Paul had read it to him even more.

Now his father was reading it to him.

She blinked. Hard.

No tears. No tears!

This is an unsentimental journey, she told herself fiercely, staring into the deepening darkness. Just come, introduce the two of them and get out of here.

So why did you tell him you'd loved him, she asked herself, sifting through the conversation she'd had with the man she was listening to.

She hadn't meant to admit that. But telling him about CJ…there hadn't seemed any way to explain her little son's existence without acknowledging love. CJ had been conceived in love and she was proud of it. The fact that Cal would never acknowledge it—that he'd admitted that the pregnancy would have seemed a disaster to him—had the potential to hurt.

It hurt now.

'The pirate's little boat started creeping out of the harbour. Creep, creep, creep.'

It was too much. Cal reading to her son. Cal reading to *his* son.

This was dangerous territory. Maybe she should leave in the morning. Fast.

The baby wasn't stable. She'd put her hand up as a cardiac expert. If she had to go in again, put more pressure on the valve…

He was too little for her to contemplate further surgery, she thought. Far, far too frail.

So what was she doing, staying here?

The baby needed her.

Right.

'"Where's my boat?" roared the pirate, and out to sea the little boat chuckled.'

Where's my plane? Gina thought. Where's my way home?

Where was home itself? She was no longer sure. She sat and tried to think about the beauty of the night, tried to think about something other than Cal—but how could she?

'Gina?' It was a yell from the far end of the path. She rose, welcoming the distraction—any distraction—and Charles was spinning down the garden path, his wheelchair moving at speed.

'Is Cal there?'

'He's inside. I'll get him.'

'I need you both.' Charles's voice was clipped and urgent. 'His damn phone's ringing out. What the hell is he thinking of, turning it off? I need him. You, too, Gina. If you'll help.'

Her heart stilled. 'The baby?'

'The baby's OK.'

That was good news. That was great news. For a moment she'd stopped breathing. But Charles was still speaking with urgency. It seemed one drama had been overtaken by another.

'Em will extend her watch and I'll take over if needed,' Charles was saying. 'But there's been a car crash.'

From through the open windows Cal had heard the medical director's voice. The pirate story had reached its conclusion. Now he appeared behind her. 'Where?' he snapped.

'Out past the O'Flattery place. The chopper's out on a call already, but it's only ten or so miles, so you can go by car. By the sound of it, kids have been drag racing. Two cars have hit head on. Deaths and multiple casualties. I've sent one car already. You'll take the second road ambulance and I'll send anyone else as they become available. Gina, it's either you or Em who has to go, and Em's concerned at Lucky's intravenous drip packing up. She's saying she has a better chance of re-establishing a line than you, and that's the biggest risk at the moment. She'll stay close and we'll set up the Theatres in readiness for what's coming. Right?'

'Right,' Gina said, dazed. 'But CJ?'

Charles was there before her. He wasn't the medical director of this place for nothing. Fast planning was what he did. 'I've asked Mrs Grubb to come across and look after the littlie,' he told her. 'If that's OK, then that leaves you free.'

'Who else is available?' Cal asked.

'Mike and Christina have taken the chopper out to pull a suspected heart case off a prawn trawler,' Charles snapped. 'It's probably a false alarm but we have to check. That's where the chopper is. Hell, Cal, weren't you listening at dinner?'

'Maybe I wasn't.'

But Charles wasn't listening now. He was focussing on Gina.

'I know we have no right to ask more of you than you've done for us already,' he told her. 'But we're desperately understaffed and we need you. Can I ask you to help?'

There was only one answer to that. 'Of course I'll help.' She was already moving toward CJ's bedroom door. 'I'll explain what's happening to CJ and come straight away.'

'He won't mind?'

'He's learned not to mind,' she said, and if her voice was bleak, who could blame her?

The ride south was at a speed which would normally have made Gina's hair curl all by itself.

Cal was driving. The first ambulance had left the moment the call had come through, the two available paramedics leaving Cal and Gina to follow. So now they followed. The siren screamed, Cal rode the corners like a racing driver and Gina gripped her seat and held on for dear life.

'Um…I have a son,' she said over the sound of the siren.

'I'm taking no risks.'

He wasn't. He was an excellent driver. He had to be. Training for remote medicine meant everyone had to be multiskilled, and the longer you stayed in the job the better you got. Cal was fantastic.

Just at the job, she told herself fiercely. Just at the job.

Charles's voice crackled from the radio. 'Cal? Gina?' Cal nodded to the receiver.

'Press the button to speak.'

She knew what to do. She'd worked with Remote Rescue before and she'd loved it. If she was to stay here there was so much she could do, she thought, and then gave herself a fast mental slap. She wasn't staying here. Why would she?

'Charles?' Back to medicine.

'The first ambulance has reached the crash site,' Charles told her, and by the tone of his voice she knew the situation was appalling. 'Two dead, seven injured, some still trapped in the wreck, and the injuries sound major. We're calling in everyone we can, but essentially you're the only two doctors available.'

'OK.' She glanced across at Cal and saw his face setting in lines of grim determination. They both knew what lay ahead.

'One of the local farmers will stay with the bodies until we can get them brought in. We'll send the chopper out as soon as we can but meanwhile use the ambulances for casualties. Let me know if I need an evacuation team from Brisbane.'

'Will do.' Any patient with trauma requiring complex intervention—such as major burns—would need to go straight to a city hospital, Gina knew. 'But you have great Theatre facilities.'

'By the sound of the injuries they may not be enough. And Cal's our only surgeon. You'll help if needed?'

'Of course.'

'Good luck, then.'

'Thanks, Charles,' she said, and replaced the receiver with a sinking heart. She glanced across at Cal again but she didn't say anything and neither did he.

He tried so hard not to care, she thought, but it didn't work. His armour was eggshell thin.

They went round a corner and she thought about where she'd left her stomach for a bit. Then they straightened and she thought about Charles. She needed some sort of diversion. Anything.

'Charles must hate that he can't come on calls like this,' she tried.

'Yeah.' Cal was concentrating fiercely on the road but it had straightened now. They were out of town, heading into flat hinterland.

'Tell me about him.' Anything to get rid of this tension, she thought, and Cal flashed her a sideways glance. He understood exactly she was doing, she realised. Maybe he even agreed with her.

'Charles is a great doctor,' he told her. 'The best. Charles's family—the Wetherbys—own a station near where you were today. Wetherby Downs. They endowed the hospital. Charles was injured when he was about eighteen—his best mate's gun went off when they were pig-shooting. Charles went to the city, learned to be a doctor and has come back and put everything he knows into this place. He's built up the best rural medical centre in Australia. The flying doctor base, the helicopter rescue service, the hospital—he runs it all and he has a mind like a steel trap.'

He hesitated for moment and Gina thought he might stop—but then his voice continued. He was staring out into the night, staring out at the road, and Gina knew he was seeing far more than the dusty track ahead.

'But I suspect on a night like tonight, Charles would change that all if he had a body that'd take him into the heart of the action,' he said slowly, reflectively. 'To be stuck back at base, waiting…'

'At least he can do something. To be injured like that, but to still go on and do something you're proud of…'

'Paul couldn't?' He asked the question gently, as if unsure that he had the right to ask, and it was her turn to stare ahead.

'The only good thing that Paul could do for the last few years was to raise CJ,' she said at last. 'Be with CJ. I kept working to support us all, but Paul was never lonely. We paid a nurse to stay during the day—but the nurse looked after Paul *and* CJ. If you know how much that helped…' She hesitated. 'Cal, that's why I'm here. It's most of the reason I've come. To tell you how grateful we both are.'

There was a moment's silence—and then a blaze of anger. She could feel it before she heard it. 'So even your husband was grateful to me. How's that supposed to make me feel?'

'I don't have a clue,' she told him honestly. 'I'm in uncharted territory. I don't even know whether I'm doing the right thing—admitting to you that CJ exists.'

'How can you question that? You should have told me five years ago.'

'You didn't want him.'

'No, but now he exists…'

She felt a tiny flare of panic. 'But now he exists, what?'

'He's my son.'

'No more than if you were a sperm donor.'

'You know it was far, far more than that.'

'Yes.' She nodded and only she knew that her hands were clenching on her lap. Her fingernails were digging into her palms and they hurt. 'Of course I know that.'

Silence. Then. 'You're planning on staying for how long?'

'Until tomorrow.'

'You need to stay longer.'

'Cal, let's not…'

'Let's not what?'

'There's no obligation on your part to care for him.'

'He looks like me.' It was a flat, inflexionless statement of fact but there was pain behind it. She could hear it.

'That's still no reason for you to be involved.'

'Dammit, Gina, he's my son.'

She thought about that while a mile—maybe two—disappeared under their wheels.

'Yes, Cal, he is,' she said at last. 'But you need to think of the whole picture. CJ's happy thinking Paul is his daddy. Are you sure you want to change that?' She hesitated. 'And I don't want to upset what's between you and Emily.'

'There's nothing between me and Emily.'

She sighed. 'Of course there's not.'

'What's that supposed to mean?'

'There's nothing between you and anyone.'

'You and I—'

'Were lovers,' she said flatly. 'But we weren't committed.'

'Because you ran.'

'I had no choice and you know it. Don't play the abandoned lover on me, Cal. You know you don't need me emotionally. You never have and you never will. And CJ…'

'What about CJ?' He was practically glowering.

'If you acknowledge him now, then you need to do commitment. There's no way you can say proudly you're his daddy and then not see him again.'

'You think that's what I want?'

'I don't know what you want. Do you?'

No answer.

Cal needed to concentrate now. They were approaching a rocky outcrop and the road was no longer clear. The country was growing rougher.

Kids were drag racing *here*? Gina thought, flinching inside at what lay ahead.

'Little fools,' Cal muttered, and she knew that his thoughts had veered back to what lay ahead as well.

'Locals, do you think?'

'Nothing surer,' he said grimly. 'There is a settlement just inland from here. Many of the local indigenous people are tribal—they live as they've lived for thousands of years. But the ones in the settlements…'

He broke off and concentrated on another corner. But then he started again.

'They're so disadvantaged,' he said savagely, and all at once his hands were white on the steering-wheel. His voice was passionate. 'Loss of their culture has left them in no man's land. There's nothing for them to look forward to, nothing for them to hold to. And they're self-destructing because of it.'

'I know,' she whispered.

'Yeah,' he said roughly. 'I remember that you do. When you were in Townsville you had such plans. You seemed to care so much. But off you went, back home to be a cardiologist.'

'That's not fair.'

But he wasn't listening. 'You know, your breakfast group disintegrated as soon as you left. The medics were stretched as far as they could go already. There was no funding and no enthusiasm for taking it forward.'

'You're blaming me that it ended?'

'You never should have started it.'

'Maybe I shouldn't have,' she said through gritted teeth.

It had been a small enough thing that she'd done. She'd taken a group of teenage girls—some pregnant, all in danger of being pregnant—and she'd invited them for breakfast. They'd met in a local café down by the river twice a week. Boys had been excluded. They'd swum, they'd eaten the huge breakfast Gina had managed to scrounge from local businesses—a breakfast of things the kids hardly saw for the rest of the week, such as milk and meat and fresh fruit. Then they'd played with cosmetics and beauty products, also provided by the businesses Gina had badgered. She'd worked really hard to keep their interest, inviting guests such as hairstylists, models, cosmeticians—anyone the girls would have thought cool.

She'd also sneaked in the odd gynaecologist and dietician and welfare support person, all selected for their cool factor as well as for the advice they'd been able to give.

The girls had thought it was wonderful—an exclusive club for twelve- to sixteen-year-olds. It had been working brilliantly, Gina thought. Too brilliantly. Only Gina knew what a pang it had cost her to walk away.

But she hadn't been alone in her enthusiasm. 'You had a boys' group,' she said softly. 'Did you walk away, too?'

'I moved up here.'

'You mean you did walk away.' She bit her lip. 'Cal, I had an excuse. I was going home to care for Paul. What about you?'

'That's none of your business.'

'No,' she whispered. She stared out into the darkness, thinking of what she and Cal had started. What they could have achieved if they'd stayed together.

Maybe Cal was right. Don't get involved.

'These kids in the crash,' she said tentatively into the silence.

'I know who'll they'll be,' he told her. 'The younger teen-agers on the settlement up here are bored stupid.'

'So bored they kill themselves?'

'They drive ancient cars. Wrecks. They get them going any way they can, and they drive like maniacs. This won't be pretty.'

'You think I don't know that?'

'I think we both know it.'

It wasn't the least bit pretty.

They rounded the last bend and knew at once what they were in for. Two cars had smashed into each other, with no last-minute swerve to lessen the impact. The vehicles were compacted, a grotesque accordion of twisted metal.

They'd have been playing chicken, Gina thought dully. She'd seen this happen before. Two carloads of kids driving straight at each other, each driver daring each other to be the last to swerve.

No one had swerved.

The first ambulance was already there and more cars were pulling up beside it. People were clutching each other, staring in horror as they stumbled out of their cars to face the crash. Bad news travelled fast. Parents would have been wrenched out of their quiet evening and were now staring at tragedy.

Two dead? There were two shrouded bundles by the road-side. A young policeman was trying fruitlessly to keep peo-ple back. Voices were already keening their sorrow, wailing distress and disbelief.

'Cal!' The older of the two paramedics who'd come with the first ambulance was running over to meet then. 'There are two still trapped in one of the cars and I'm scared we're los-ing them. And there's a kid on the roadside with major breath-ing problems. Plus the rest.'

'You take the breathing,' Cal told Gina. 'I'll take the car.'

He was bracing himself. Gina could see it. His eyes were withdrawing into the place he kept his pain. He'd do his job with efficiency and skill, and he'd care while he worked, but he'd not let himself become involved.

'I'll do whatever needs doing,' she said, in a voice that wasn't too steady. 'But maybe I'll feel pain along the way.'

'And I won't?'

'Who knows?' She was hauling on protective gear with speed. 'I knew this job once, and I thought I knew you. But we've come a long way. How thick have you grown your armour now, Cal?'

She didn't wait for an answer.

It was a night to forget.

Gina worked with skills she'd almost forgotten, but her skills returned because if they didn't then kids died.

The girl with breathing problems appeared to have fractured ribs, with a possible punctured lung. She was Gina's first priority. Gina set up oxygen and manoeuvred her into a position where she seemed to be a good colour with normal oxygen saturation. She left her with the younger paramedic—Frank—and moved on to the next priority.

There were fractured limbs, deep lacerations, shock… That was bad enough, but Cal had allocated himself the true horror. Two kids still trapped.

One of them died under his hands five minutes after they arrived.

There was a moment's appalled silence—a moment where she glanced across and saw Cal's shoulders slump in defeat and despair—and then they all had to keep working.

How thick was his armour? she wondered. Not thick enough.

Head-on smash. Three dead now. One dreadfully injured. Three more with severe injuries, some of those injuries requiring skills that weren't available in Crocodile Creek. One in such deep shock that she wasn't responding.

There was a girl still trapped in the car. Cal was in the car with her, somehow inching his body into the mass of tangled metal, and he was fighting with everything he had.

All the emergency services had arrived now and machinery was being prepared to slice the cars apart. When floodlights lit the scene Gina saw that Cal was holding a tracheostomy tube in place. The second paramedic, Mario, was helping. IV lines had been established. A tow-truck driver had been co-opted into being a human intravenous stand.

She worked on. She had too many troubles of her own to be distracted by what Cal was doing.

'Dr Lopez?' Gina was splinting a compound fracture that was threatening to block blood supply when suddenly Mario was kneeling beside her. The too-young paramedic had the horror of the night etched on his face, but he was competent, moving swiftly to take over.

'I can do this,' he told her. She had the boy's leg in position and was about to start binding. 'Dr Jamieson needs you over at the car. Can you go?'

'Sure.'

Do what comes next, Gina thought bleakly, trying not to flinch as she approached the wreck. Do what comes next.

Cal's patient—Karen, a girl of about fourteen—was still firmly trapped and she wasn't moving. The guys with the cutting machinery had paused.

Why did Cal need her?

She did a fast visual assessment of what she could see. Massive facial damage. What else?

'Her leg,' Cal told her as she reached him. 'I can't reach and I can feel blood. It was oozing, but we shifted her a bit when we tried to free her and now it's spurting. Mario tried to get in but he can't reach under me and I can't move. You're smaller. If we don't get the bleeding stopped…'

She didn't answer. She was already bending into the mass of twisted metal, crawling under Cal's legs.

Someone—Frank?—handed her a torch.

'There's a tear.' She could see it. 'It's pumping. I want pressure.'

Frank pushed a pad in her hands.

'Can you stop it?' The fear in Cal's voice was unmistakable. Armour? He didn't have any at all, she thought. It was all a façade.

She was right underneath him, her body somehow under his legs. There were pieces of metal digging into her from all sides as she bound the leg as best she could, hauling the jagged sides together and dressing it so the worst of the bleeding eased.

But had the bleeding eased because of what she'd done— or because the girl's blood pressure had dropped so far the bleeding would have eased anyhow?

She wriggled back out, but she didn't ask the question.

'We'll be getting you out of here now,' Cal was murmuring to the girl, holding her as he supported the tracheostomy tube, his arm around her shoulders, willing her to hear him. She seemed unconscious but both of them knew there was no way they could assess her level of consciousness here. She might well be able to hear every word.

Gina stepped back, but her eyes stayed on Karen's face. Was this a winnable battle? From what she could see, no.

But Cal wasn't giving up.

'OK, guys,' Cal was saying to the men working around them. 'Now Gina's fixed the bleeding, there's nothing stopping us cutting her out. Karen, we're with you every step of the way. Gina and I won't leave you.'

Gina and I.

Gina backed, moving out of the way of the men with the machinery, but the image of the girl Cal was treating stayed with her. The girl's pupils weren't responding to light. Her face was badly damaged, and there was a deep indentation behind her ear. Fractured skull. What damage was underneath?

Cal wasn't moving clear. The cars were having to be wrenched apart to get her out. There'd be splintering of metal; there was danger in him staying where he was. It was probably a hopeless task—but he wouldn't leave.

Gina and I.

She loved him. He was so desperately needful and she loved him so much, but he wouldn't see it.

Numbly she went back to the kids who still needed her. Her girl with the punctured lung seemed to be stabilising. The boy with fractured legs was drifting into unconsciousness but part of that might well be the morphine she'd administered. The girl who seemed to be in deep shock wasn't taking anything in, and Frank called her over to help. She went, but a part of her stayed achingly with Cal holding the girl to him, fighting against all odds.

Cal battling the odds as he'd done all his life.

Medicine. Concentrate on need.

'The chopper's on its way,' one of the policemen told her.

That meant she could arrange to get the girl with the punctured lung and the one in shock into the road ambulance. She sent them off with the two paramedics. They'd need the helicopter for Karen. If…

If.

The vast pliers-like equipment nicknamed the Jaws of Life was working now, the noise blocking out any other. It stopped for a minute and she heard Cal.

'Breathe for me, Karen. Come on, love. Breathe.'

Love. He was fighting with love, she thought, and he didn't even know he was doing it.

She needed time to think things through.

There was no time here.

Then the helicopter landed, and Gina was so busy she hardly noticed. One of the boys was vomiting and it took all her skill to stop him choking. She had him on his side, clearing his airway, and when Cal's hand settled on her shoulder she jerked back in surprise.

He was clear of the wreck, but she glanced up and saw that he wasn't clear. Karen…

Not dead. Not yet.

Cal was looking at the boys she was treating, doing fast visual assessment, trying to figure priorities.

'I'll take Karen back to base in the chopper,' he said, briefly, dully, as if he was already accepting the outcome. 'Her parents will want to come with us, and by the look of…things, I think that's wise.' He stooped to feel the pulse of the boy who'd just vomited. Both boys were seriously injured but not so seriously that their lives were in immediate danger. But both of them needed constant medical attention. It wasn't safe to leave either without a doctor.

Which left them with a dilemma. Only one of these kids could fit in the two-patient chopper, but if one of them went, Cal's attention would be divided. Or Gina would need to go, too, leaving one boy untended.

Impossible. They'd have to wait.

'I'll send the chopper straight back,' Cal told her, and she understood.

'Fine.'

Fine? To be left on the roadside with three dead kids and two seriously injured kids and so many distraught relatives?

'No one else can stay,' Cal told her helplessly. 'Damn, there should be another doctor. We're so short-staffed.'

'Just go, Cal,' she told him. 'Move.'

'I'll send someone back to cope with the deaths,' Cal said. There were adults keening over the bodies and the scene looked like something out of a nightmare. Worse than a nightmare. 'Charles said he'd send back-up. Where is it? But, Gina, I need to go.'

'Of course you do. Go, Cal. I'll manage.'

He touched her hair, a fleeting gesture of farewell—but then, before she could begin to guess what he intended, he bent and kissed her. Hard. It was a swift kiss that held more desperation than tenderness. It was a kiss of pure, desperate need.

Maybe it had been intended as reassurance for her, she thought numbly as she raised a hand to her face, but it had ended up being a kiss for himself. For Cal.

Cal had never kissed her as he'd just done then.

But he was already gone, stepping away from her. Stepping away from his need.

Into the chopper, back into his medicine, and away from her.

Somehow she organised order from the chaos at the roadside. She couldn't work miracles—there were still three dead kids. But she sent relatives to start the drive into town so they could be at the hospital when the kids were brought in. She worked with the police sergeant who'd come to assist the white-faced officers who'd been first on the scene, getting details from shocked relatives. The bodies had to stay where they were until the coroner arrived.

She worked.

Finally the helicopter returned and by the time it did, she had her two remaining patients ready to go. She'd hauled the stretchers from the road ambulance she and Cal had come in, so the moment the chopper landed she had them ready to carry on board. Mike was the pilot. He swung out to help her. There was another paramedic or doctor in the back, receiving the patients, but there was no time for introductions.

'Let's go,' Mike told her.

She glanced one last time at the mess left for the police to handle—the detritus of wasted lives—and then she concentrated on the living. She climbed up into the chopper herself. Moving on.

If only it was that easy.

Someone—a big man with a Scottish accent that was apparent the moment he opened his mouth—was organising the securing of the stretchers. He talked over his shoulder to Gina as Mike fastened himself back into the pilot's seat.

'You'll be Gina,' he said briefly, hanging the boy's drip from the stand built into the side of the chopper. 'I'm Dr Hamish McGregor. Call me Hamish.'

'William's IV line's not stable. And his leg…'

'I'm noticing that, and it's my problem.' Hamish was making a calm assessment of each patient. And of her. 'You look like death and I'm taking over. If I need you, I'll say so. Meanwhile, sit back and close your eyes.'

'But—'

'Just do it.'

She did. She buckled her seat belt and closed her eyes, and suddenly nausea washed over her in a wave so intense that she needed to push her head down between her knees to stop herself passing out.

Hamish eyed her with concern but he left her to it. Every doctor in the world had these moments. They came with the job.

So for a while Gina simply concentrated on not giving way to horror. On not letting the dizziness take over.

Finally, though, the nausea passed. She took a few deep breaths and ventured—cautiously—to open her eyes again. The helicopter was in the air. The two kids seemed settled and Hamish was focussing on her.

'So you're Cal's Gina,' he said softly.

'I… No.'

'No?'

'I'm just a doctor tonight,' she said wearily, and then, because she couldn't think of what else to say, she added, 'Where's Cal?'

'Last time I saw him he was about to drill a burrhole to try and relieve raised cranial pressure,' he told her. 'It's desperate surgery he's doing. We're damnably short-staffed. Every doctor at the base is doing two jobs or more tonight.'

'So where did you come from?'

The big Scot managed a lopsided smile. 'I'm supposed to be on leave,' he told her. 'However, I made the mistake of telling people where I was. Charles radioed the skipper of the game-fishing boat I was on and they hauled me back to town with the boating equivalent of red lights and sirens. To be met by this.'

'So you're another doctor with the Remote Rescue Service.' She frowned. 'Hamish. The paediatrician?'

'Yes, ma'am.' He gave a rueful smile. 'Or I'm the best we can supply in the paediatric department. I have a post-grad qualification in paediatrics, as well as my accident and emergency training.'

Great. That was another small weight lifted from her heart. All the time she'd been out here she'd been conscious of the tiny baby she'd left back at base, and now they had someone with paediatric training to take over. 'You've seen Lucky?'

'I have,' he told her. 'He's looking stable. I'll be heading back there fast to spend some more time with him. But you and Cal and Emily seem to have done a fine job. He has a fighting chance.'

'I would have thought you'd have stayed while Em came out,' she said, puzzled, and he grimaced.

'Em's in Theatre with Cal. He needs the best anaesthetist we have. Christina and Charles are with the two kids who arrived by road. That means we're right out of doctors—apart from Alix, our pathologist, who's just recovering from chickenpox. And we've even pulled her out of bed. So we had to take a chance on Lucky. Grace is specialling him. I came here. Sometimes in this place there's not enough skill to go around and you need to make a hard call.'

'I guess,' she said, thinking bleakly of the number of times

she'd had to leave her own son as she was leaving him now.
As she'd have to walk away from Cal. So many choices…

Think of something else, she told herself fiercely.
Anything.

'Do you know Cal well?'

'Cal's a friend.'

'I didn't think Cal had friends.' Why was she asking this,
she wondered, in the midst of this horror? But the boys they
were transporting now were the least injured. They were heavily sedated and they both had parents gripping their undam-
aged hands, as if that link alone could keep them safe. There
was time and space for the two medics to talk.

And surprisingly Gina found she wanted to talk. In truth, she
was desperate to talk. Anything but face the horrors of the night.

Anything but Cal?

But she'd asked.

'Our Cal certainly keeps to himself,' Hamish was saying.
He cast an assessing look across at their patients but it appeared their respite could continue. 'But… Gina, there's things
going on that I'm not understanding. I was barely back in town
for two minutes before I was told you've produced Cal's son.
Cal's son! Would that be right? Have you done that?'

'Yes. But I'll take him away again,' Gina whispered. 'I just
wanted Cal to know he was alive. You don't think I'm intend-
ing to cut in on his precious independence, do you?'

His eyes grew thoughtful. 'You know,' he said softly, 'it
wouldn't be such a bad thing if you did.'

'He's getting along fine without me,' Gina snapped. 'He's
got a relationship with Emily.'

'Has he, now?' Hamish sent another assessing look across
at their patients but both boys were breathing deep and evenly
and there was no need to worry. One of the fathers had his
head on his son's hand, as if love alone could bring him
through. 'I wasn't aware that he had such a thing,' Hamish said

softly. 'And I know both Emily and Cal very well. Cal doesn't have a relationship with anyone.'

'But I thought… On the day I arrived here I found him… cuddling Emily.'

Hamish thought about that for a bit. 'Emily's fiancé has just walked out on her,' he said at last. 'He's saying he wants space, but in reality he's found another woman. Em knows in her heart what's happening, no matter how much she's denying it. If Cal was cuddling Emily, I'd be guessing that it was just Cal picking up the pieces.' He hesitated. 'You know, picking up the pieces is what Cal's best at,' he remarked thoughtfully. 'It's what to do with them afterwards where he doesn't exactly shine.'

Gina blinked, and stared. Astonished. 'You're a paediatrician,' she said slowly. 'Not a psychiatrist.'

'Everyone does everything at Crocodile Creek,' Hamish told her, giving her a rueful smile. 'There's no such thing as delineation of roles. If we need a psychiatrist then I'll be one. And I do consider Cal a friend. Even if it is a bit one-sided, if you know what I mean.' He cast her a long, questioning look. 'And I'm imagining you know very well what I mean.'

They fell into silence again. So much had happened in the last few hours. This sort of life-and-death drama always left her drained, Gina thought wearily, and tonight was no exception. She was exhausted. In a few minutes they'd land and they'd be thrust back into the hospital atmosphere where there'd be surgery to perform, appalled relatives to counsel and treat, Cal to face…

This was her two minutes to catch her breath and look squarely at her future.

She couldn't. Cal…

'I don't know what to do,' she whispered, and Hamish had to lean forward to hear. 'I don't know how to break through that barrier.'

'It's one heck of a barrier,' Hamish told her. 'You know his family history.'

'I know what I've been allowed to know.'

'He's been betrayed by just about everybody in his life. It's a miracle he's a functioning human being.'

'He's not a trusting human being. So that makes him…'

'Dysfunctional?'

'Maybe,' she whispered. 'Yes.'

'Then how far are you prepared to go to get him functioning again?' Hamish asked, and Gina stared at the metal-plated floor and shook her head.

'Not far at all. I'm just here to tell him of the existence of his son.'

'You know, I doubt that,' Hamish said gently. 'I've known you, what—for about fifteen minutes? And even now, I doubt that very much.'

She'd been right when she'd assumed the hospital would be in chaos. The casualty entrance was mad.

Gina stood between the two stretchers that had just been wheeled in and took three deep breaths, trying for triage, trying to get some sort of priorities formed in her head. Grace appeared in the doorway, looking just as frazzled as she was feeling.

'Where is everyone?' Gina demanded.

'Both Theatres are occupied,' Grace said briefly. 'Karen's intracranial pressure is life-threatening. She has signs of a blood clot in association with her fractured skull and Cal's drilled a burrhole to try and reduce pressure. Melanie has a collapsed lung and Christina and Charles are working on her. Alix is looking after path. needs and blood supply. That's taken our full complement of doctors, except you and Hamish. Hamish, you need to check on Lucky. I came out to see if you needed any help here.' She gazed around the mess that was the emergency ward. 'I guess you do, huh?'

'I guess we do,' Gina said, mentally saying goodbye to the rest of the night. What a day. What a nightmare! 'I guess we all do.'

They worked for two hours straight. Evacuation in the morning would see the compound fractures taken to Cairns for attention by orthopaedic specialists, but meanwhile blood supply had to be ensured, adequate pain relief had to be given, wounds had to be stitched. With only paramedics and nurses to help her, Gina had three incredibly sick and traumatised kids in her care. To say nothing of their parents.

But somehow she coped, and when Charles finally arrived to take over she was able to greet the medical director with a faint smile of reassurance.

Charles's face twisted as he looked around the room. She had each patient settled and ready to be transferred to the wards—or to a flight out. Their appropriate relatives were settled with them. The inappropriate relatives or the onlookers who were simply there for drama had been sent home.

'Is everything OK?' he asked.

'I'll go through the case notes—'

'There's no need,' Charles told her. Christina appeared in the doorway behind him and the complement of doctors had suddenly grown to three. Charles spun across to the desk and lifted the folders she'd started out at the crash site. 'Christina and I can take over here.'

'Lilly?'

'She'll be fine,' Christina told her. 'We'll fly her out for plastic surgery tomorrow morning but she's stable.'

'And… Karen…?'

'That's your next job,' Charles said grimly. 'I'm sorry, Gina, but I can't let you go to bed yet.'

'You need help with Karen?'

'Karen died twenty minutes ago,' Charles told her. 'Cal and

Emily worked with everything they had, but they failed. Cal's just talked to her parents.' He hesitated. 'Gina, when things like this happen, Cal withdraws. He's out in the hospital garden right now, and he needs someone.'

She stared at him, appalled. 'What are you asking? I don't… I can't…'

'Yes, you can,' he told her, and his voice became stern. 'You've thrown a hell of a shock at our Cal this afternoon. The least you can do is mop up the mess.'

'It's nothing to do with me.'

'Who are you kidding?' he said roughly. 'But you choose. Go to bed or go and see if you can get through to Cal. But if you go to bed now…well, I don't see how you can.' He stared around the room and his face grew even more grim. 'There are things that all of us can't walk away from. You know that as well as everyone here.'

CHAPTER FIVE

SHE should go to bed. She'd do more harm than good if she approached Cal now, she thought, and CJ needed her. She made her way resolutely across to the doctors' quarters, avoiding the garden, sure that she'd made the right decision.

CJ wasn't in bed. Instead, there was a note pinned to his pillow.

Dear Dr Lopez

CJ couldn't sleep and he seems a bit upset. We've got a new puppy at our place. Me and Mr Grubb are in the little blue house over the far side of the hospital and hubby's just come over to tell me the pup's making a fuss. So I thought I'd take CJ home. I'm guessing he and the pup might sleep together in our spare bedroom. I asked Dr Wetherby and he reckons you'll be busy till late and us taking the littlie will give you a chance to sleep late tomorrow—but come over and get him if you want him back tonight. Or telephone and we'll bring him straight back. I'll let you know if he frets.

Dora Grubb

So CJ didn't need her, Gina thought as she stared down at the letter. This was a note written by a competent woman who

Charles trusted. CJ would be overjoyed to be asked to sleep with a puppy.

But where did that leave her?

She wanted to hug CJ, she thought bleakly, acknowledging that her ability to hug her small son in times of crisis was a huge gift. But to wake him now, to wake the Grubbs and the puppy as well, just so she could be hugged...

Grow up, she told herself, and tried to feel grown-up.

She glanced at her watch. It was three in the morning. She should shower and slide between the covers and sleep.

She knew she wouldn't sleep.

Damn, she wanted CJ.

Cal was... Cal was...

Go to bed!

She took a grip—sort of—and walked over to pull the curtains closed. Then she paused.

Cal was down at the water's edge. The shoreline was two hundred yards from where she was standing but his figure was unmistakable.

He was just...standing.

So what? she demanded of herself. She should leave him be.

But he was Cal. She stared down the beach at his still figure and she felt the same wrenching of her heart that she'd felt all those years before. It was as if this man was a part of her and to walk away from him would be tantamount to taking away a limb.

She'd had to walk away before, she thought dully, for all sorts of reasons. And she'd survived.

But CJ was safely asleep and there was nothing standing between herself and Cal.

Nothing but five years of pain, and a desolate childhood that had destroyed his trust in everyone.

He'd never get over it, she told herself. He was damaged goods. Dangerous.

But still she couldn't walk away. Not now. There was only so much resolve one woman was capable of, and she'd run right out of it.

She opened her door and she walked down to the beach to meet him.

He sensed rather that saw her approach. What was it about this woman that gave him a sixth sense—that made him feel different, strange, just because she was on the same continent as he was? he wondered. She was walking along the beach to reach him and he braced himself as if expecting to be hit.

She'd hurt him.

No, he'd hurt her, he thought savagely. She'd been pregnant and he hadn't been there for her.

He would have been there if she'd said…

Liar. He would have run.

'I'm sorry, Cal,' she said gently behind him, and he flinched. But he didn't turn.

'What do you want?' It was a low growl. He sounded angry, which was grossly unfair but he was past being fair tonight.

Maybe she sensed it. She sounded softly sympathetic—not responding with her own anger.

'It's been a dreadful day, Cal. To have CJ thrown at you, and then copping such deaths…'

'I couldn't save her,' he said savagely into the night. He'd left his shoes back on the dry sand and rolled up his jeans before he'd come down the water's edge. The water was now washing over his feet, taking out some of the heat but not enough. Still he didn't turn and Gina came and stood beside him and stared out at the same sea he was seeing. She was wearing jeans and T-shirt and sandals, but she didn't seem to notice that she was wading into the shallows regardless. Neither did he. 'I worked so damned hard and I couldn't save her. Of all the useless…'

'You can only do so much, Cal. You're a doctor. Not a magician.'

'The pressure was too much,' he said, picking up a ribbon of kelp that had washed against his legs and hurling it into an oncoming breaker. It didn't go far. He walked further into the waves to retrieve it and then hurled it again. 'Did you know we actually split her skull, trying to save her?' he demanded. 'We drilled a burrhole, but the whole brain was so bruised we realised the pressure was killing her. So we split…'

Gina was beside him—but not too close. They were up to their knees in the surf and the rolling breakers were reaching their thighs. She didn't touch him. They were standing three feet apart, and she was staring out to sea, and he knew that she was seeing what he was seeing. A dying child.

'That's heroic surgery, Cal,' she said softly. 'Performed as a last-ditch stand in a hopeless case. But it was hopeless. You can't blame yourself when something like that doesn't work. Medicine has limits.'

'Yeah.'

She took a step closer and laid a hand on his arm. He flinched.

'Don't.'

'Don't touch you, do you mean?' she asked. 'Cal, that's what you've been saying for years. You're so afraid of people being close.'

'What do you know about what I'm like now?'

'Hamish says your friendship with Emily is platonic,' she murmured softly, and her hand stayed on his arm, whether he willed it or not. 'He says you're still driving people away.'

'I didn't drive you away.'

'No?'

'Gina—'

'OK, let's leave it,' she told him, her voice softening in sympathy. But instead of removing her hand from his arm, she linked her fingers through his and tugged him sideways. Cal had such shadows but he'd earned them the hard way. For him to move past them must be a near-impossible task. 'Let's leave the lid on it.'

'What are…?' She was tugging him through the shallows. 'Where—?'

'Cal, there's one thing I have learned in the last few years,' she told him, still tugging so he had no option but to follow. 'Reinforced by stuff like tonight. And that's the reality that you can't spend your life dwelling in the shadows of what's gone. If you do that, then you might as well finish it off when you lose the ones you love. But I only have one life, Cal. I intend to make the most of it.'

'So what's that—?'

'It means I'm going for a walk in the moonlight,' she told him, refusing to let him interrupt. 'CJ's safe with Mrs Grubb and the new Grubb puppy. This water is delicious. It's a full moon and it's low tide. We have miles of beach all to ourselves and there's no way either of us is going to sleep after today's events. So let's walk.'

He stopped. Firm. Planting his feet in the shallows. Holding himself still against the insistent tug of her hand.

'I don't think that's a good idea.'

'I think it's a splendid idea,' she told him, sounding exasperated.

'I don't want to get close to you, Gina.'

'You know, I have news for you,' she told him, linking her arm through his and keeping on tugging. 'You're the father of my son. You're here now. You don't want to get close? Cal Jamieson, you already are.'

He was walking. Gina started down the beach through the shallows, and Cal let himself be tugged beside her, and as he relaxed and started to walk without being tugged she knew she'd achieved a significant victory.

He'd always taken deaths personally, she thought. It was one of the things she loved about him. Most doctors developed personal detachment from patients, but she'd never seen that in Cal, no matter how hard he fought to find it.

He'd never succeeded in personal detachment. Except in his personal relationships.

Except with her.

But for now he was walking beside her, fighting the way he was feeling about her and about CJ, and at least that meant that he wasn't internalising Karen's death, she thought. The hours after such a death were always dreadful. Going over and over things in your mind, wondering what else could you have done, what you'd missed…

She could distract him for a little while, she thought, and if by doing so she could distract herself from…things, great.

Or at least good.

Given the staffing in the hospital, they both knew they couldn't venture far, so they confined their walk to the end of the cove. But as they reached the headland, Gina decided it was not far enough. So they walked to the opposite headland. Then they turned again—and again. Walking in silence.

So many things unsaid.

'We'll wear the beach out,' Cal told her, breaking the silence on their third turn, and Gina kicked up a spray of water in front of her and smiled.

'Good. I like my beach a little world-weary. You have no idea how much I miss the beach.'

'So where are you living?' It was almost a normal conversation, Gina thought. Excellent.

'Idaho. Same as when you first knew me, Cal. Some things don't change.'

'But you love the beach.'

'Mmm, but my family and friends are in Idaho. So sure I miss the beach but where I live is a no-brainer.'

'You always intended to go back?' he asked, and she felt the normality fade as anger surged again. Deep anger. This water wasn't cold enough.

'Strangely enough, I didn't,' she told him. 'Five years ago I came out for a break after Paul left me. Yes, I intended it to be brief, but then I met you. And then I thought about staying permanently.'

'So you considered deserting your family and friends.'

'I had hoped,' she said softly, 'that in you I might have found both. I was dumb. But I was young, Cal. I've learned. So it's back to Idaho for me.'

'You must know that I'll want to see CJ.'

'I'll send photographs.'

'I didn't mean that.'

'So what do you mean?'

'I don't know,' he said, exasperated. 'He's my kid.'

She thought about that for a minute, trying to figure out a response that didn't involve anger. 'Do you think,' she said softly into the night, 'that because your mother and your father were your biological parents, they had automatic rights over you?'

'Not rights,' he said, in an automatic rejection of an idea he clearly found repugnant, and she grimaced.

'No. They had obligations, which they didn't fulfil. But rights... You have to earn rights. If you love your kid then maybe you have the right to hope the kid will love you back. You're at first base, Cal.'

'He looks like me,' Cal said inconsequentially, and his words sent a surge of disquiet through her. Like something was being threatened. Her relationship with CJ?

'So do you love him?' she managed to ask, and he seemed startled.

'Hey...'

She kicked up a huge spray of water before her, so high it

came back down over their heads. Enough. This conversation was way too deep and she didn't know where it was going, and she wasn't sure how she could handle it wherever it went. And she was so tired. She kicked again and then suddenly on impulse she dropped Cal's hand and waded further out into the sea. Her clothes were already wet. They were disgusting anyway after this night, so a little more salt water wasn't going to hurt them. The moon was so full that she could see under the surface of the shallow water and…and what the heck.

Walking forward to the first breaker, she simply knelt down and let the water wash right over her.

It felt excellent. Her anger, her uncertainty, the way she was feeling about Cal…the way her hand had felt as if it was abandoning something precious when she'd released Cal's. The waves had the power to soothe it all.

This had been some day. The trauma of the baby, and then the accident, and Cal as well. It was simply, suddenly over-whelming. Now her brain seemed to have shut down as her body soaked in the cool wash of the foam. She knelt and let wave after wave wash over her and she just didn't care.

She didn't know where to go from here.

She wasn't sure how long she knelt there, how long was it before she surfaced to the awareness that Cal was still with her. He was kneeling behind her. A wave washed her backwards and his hands seized her waist so that she wasn't washed under.

Maybe he'd sensed that she'd reached a limit where it was no longer possible to support herself, she thought dully in the tiny part of her mind that was still capable of thought.

Or maybe he needed contact, too?

It didn't matter. It couldn't matter, for there was no space in her tired mind to make any sense of anything. She was grate-ful that he was here and she leaned back into him but still her focus was on the water, on the wash of cool, on this minute.

'The sea's great,' Cal murmured during a break in the

waves, and she thought about answering but another wave washed up against her and she had to concentrate on getting her breath back. She spluttered a bit and thought, Well, that served her right for trying to think of something clever to say. Of anything to say.

'Where do you go in Idaho when you feel like this?' he asked some time later, and that was a reasonable question to ask, she decided. There was no danger down that road.

'I drive,' she told him. 'The night Paul died I got in the car and I drove and drove. A friend took CJ home with her for the night and I think I drove five hundred miles before I stopped.'

'I wish I'd known.'

'Do you?' she asked. She tried to shrug but his hold on her waist tightened.

'Believe it or not, yes, I do,' he said softly.

'Your friend Hamish said you were really good at picking up the pieces,' she murmured. 'He also said you didn't know what to do with them after you've picked them up.'

'He's got me tagged.' But he didn't sound angry. He sounded defeated.

'I guess he's a friend.'

A wave or two more washed over them and they had to wait for a bit before they could talk again. But she was feeling the tension in him and it wasn't going away.

'Does Hamish being my friend give him permission to talk about me?' he asked at last.

She thought, No, this wasn't about Hamish. But she answered him all the same.

'It gives him permission to worry about you. Like with kids, commitment gives rights.'

'Hell, Gina...'

'Just leave it, Cal,' she said wearily. She tried to pull away but another wave, bigger than usual, propelled her harder against him. His arm tightened even further.

'I don't think I can,' he said unsteadily.

'We need to go back to the hospital.'

'We have unfinished business.'

'I can't think what.' She tried to sound cross—but it didn't come off.

'Gina…' Things had changed suddenly. The feel of his hands. The feel of his body…

Once she and Cal had been lovers and suddenly the feel of his hands touching her had brought it all flooding back. The way she'd once felt about this man.

The way she still did.

Cal. He was her Cal. She'd fallen desperately in love with him five years ago. She'd spent five years trying to forget how he felt but now all he had to do was be here, touch her, and it was as if those feelings had started yesterday.

No. Not yesterday. Now.

And he could feel it, too. She half turned and he was looking down at her in the moonlight, the expression on his face something akin to amazement.

What was between them wasn't one-sided. It was a real and tangible bond, and five years hadn't weakened it one bit.

'Cal, don't,' she whispered, but it was a shaken whisper.

'How can I not?'

She should have struggled.

Of course she should have struggled. She didn't want this man to kiss her.

She mustn't let him kiss her. To rekindle what had once been…

But she was so tired. The part of her brain that was used for logic had simply switched off, stopped with its working out of what she should do, what was wise, what the best path was to the future.

All she knew was that Cal's closeness, the feel of his hands on her body, the sensation of his mouth lowering onto hers, was transporting her into another space.

Another time?

Five years ago.

She knew this man. She'd fallen in love with Cal Jamieson the first time he'd smiled at her. She'd told herself it was crazy, that love at first sight was ridiculous, that she wasn't even divorced yet—but it had made no difference at all.

This was her man. Her home. He was the Adam to her Eve, the other half of her whole, her completeness.

Six, seven years ago Paul had walked away from their marriage because he'd sensed that there had been something more. She'd been devastated. She hadn't understood.

And then she'd met Cal and all had become clear.

Paul had been right. That it had gone so horribly wrong for them both hadn't been Paul's fault. He'd gone in search of something he'd sensed had been out there. He'd been injured before he'd found it, but Gina had found it here.

Cal.

She was holding him tight. Tighter.

What was it between them? She didn't know. Pure, uncomplicated lust? There was certainly that, she thought. Her body was reacting to his as if there was some switch that sent heat surging in a way she hadn't felt for five long years.

He made her feel…

What?

Who was asking for explanations? Why waste this moment? She surely wasn't going to.

Her lips opened to his and she hadn't wanted to be kissed— or she was almost sure she hadn't wanted to be kissed—but she was numb and past rational thought and she was wet and his body was so close and their clothes were soaked, so soaked that they might as well not have existed, and his hands were wonderful and she could taste him and she was sinking against him and…

And he was her Cal.

The heat was overpowering. She was melting inside, turning to liquid jelly as wave after wave of pure hot longing surged through her body. She was responding to him with every nerve ending she had, from the tips of her ears to the tips of her toes. The waves were washing against them and at times they were up to their necks in the water, but it made it more wonderful. It didn't take away the heat.

Nothing could take away this heat.

'Gina…'

He was holding her close. Closer. She was merging into him under the water, her body curling against him as if two melting objects were merging into one. Her lips widened, her tongue was searching… She wanted this man so much.

The kiss deepened, lengthened, strengthened, and with it came a strengthening of the bond that had been forged five years ago. It was a bond she'd thought she'd broken but she knew now that she never could.

This man was her son's father.

This man was her love.

But he didn't know it. Not as she wanted him to know it, in a glorious acknowledgement that they could be a family.

'You're beautiful,' he managed in a voice that was husky with passion. She'd drawn away as a wave had crashed against them but he'd tugged her back into him again and she had no power to resist.

'You're not so bad yourself,' she whispered, before his mouth lowered again. She even managed a shaken laugh. 'A bit soggy…'

'Soggy's good. Soggy's great.'

'Shut up and kiss me, Cal.'

'Yes, ma'am.'

What was she doing? she wondered in the tiny fraction of her brain available for such thought. But she knew very well what she was doing. She was taking what was offered right now because this moment was all she had. Even if Cal wanted to forge something from now on, there was no way he was offering himself. He'd hold himself independent, regardless. He'd drilled that hard lesson into his heart and he intended to stay that way.

But just for now, just for this minute, she told herself desperately, there was no such thing as independence. Cal was a part of her and she'd take what comfort she could before she moved on.

Tomorrow.

For some reason the word slammed through her tired brain, smashing against the love and the heat and the joy, and she felt her body shudder. He felt it, as he'd feel a wave crashing against them, and he drew away again, holding her at arm's length and looking at her in concern.

'What is it, my love?'

Doctor picking up pieces, she thought dully. Then not knowing what to do with them. Cal would always act with honour. He was so kind, so caring…

He just couldn't take the next step.

'I'm not your love,' she said, in a voice that was none too steady.

'I've loved you from the first time we met.'

'Have you?'

'Of course I have.'

But the bubble had burst. Reality was slamming back and with it a kind of sense.

'Then what, Cal?' she said, knowing exactly where this was headed. 'What? If you do indeed love me, then what? Do you want us to stay together?'

His face shuttered. 'Don't, Gina,' he whispered. 'Not yet. I can't. Just let's take this moment.'

'Like we did five years ago? That ended up with CJ.'

Where had that come from? She hadn't wanted to say it. This moment could well be all she had, and to spoil it…

But desire was being replaced by an anger that couldn't be ignored.

'I'm not suggesting we go to bed,' he told her, and her anger grew.

'Good. Neither am I.'

'We have to figure something out.'

This was ridiculous. They were chest-deep in water, discussing their future. Or their lack of a future. The waves were washing in and out, Cal's hands still held her firm around the waist, protecting her from the waves' force, and she was so close. But his face, his eyes…they said there was still a distance between them.

Of course there was a distance between them.

'Gina, do you have to go back to the States?' he asked, and she stilled.

'What are you suggesting?'

'We need to work things out.'

'Maybe.' Be careful, her head was screaming. Be very careful. But there was a tiny hope…

'Gina, you loved working in Townsville.'

So I did, she thought. Because you were there.

'What if I did?' she asked, and managed to keep her voice steady.

'You had your kids' club. You enjoyed it. You loved the emergency work.'

'That's right.'

'If you were to go back there… Townsville's only an hour's flight from here. I spend a lot of time there.'

The world seemed to have stopped breathing. She tried to make herself think. 'So…why would I go to Townsville?'

'I could see you,' he told her. 'I work a roster of three

weeks on, one week off. I could spend a week at Townsville and get to know CJ.'

'I guess you could.' Her glimmer of hope had faded into nothing. Her voice sounded leaden, defeated. What else had she expected? she asked of herself. Fairy-tales were for storybooks. Not for her. 'But where would that leave me?'

'You liked Townsville.'

'My family and friends are in Idaho.'

'I'd be in Townsville.'

'Once a month.'

'Gina, we could see how it went.' His voice was softly persuasive and he bent to kiss her again.

But she was having none of it and she shoved him away.

'Yes, we could,' she said. Anger was her only aid now, but she had it in spades. More than anger. Pure, blind fury. 'I could give up my very good job in the States. I could abandon my friends. But why, Cal? So you get to see CJ once a month?'

'He's my son.'

'Prove it,' she snapped. 'What makes a father? A one-night stand?'

'We never had a one-night stand. You know that.'

'I know it. Do you?'

'Gina, I'm saying that I've loved you.' He put a hand through his sodden hair, raking it with the air of a man past his limits. He was as exhausted as she was, she thought, and had to fight an almost overwhelming compulsion to reach out to him. But no way. No way! 'These last few years have been hell.'

'But not enough to reach out now and say let's be a family. Not enough to even want me to stay in the same town as you.'

'I don't do—'

'You don't do commitment,' she finished for him, almost cordially. 'So what's new?'

'You know as well as I do what happens down that road,' he told her, and he was drawing away from her now. 'Look at what happened tonight. One minute these people had loving, laughing teenagers, the next they had nothing. You had Paul and he's dead. And me… I learned that lesson over and over again. The only way of sanity is independence. You can love someone and stay independent. You must.'

'Can you? Can you really love them?'

'That's what I'm saying,' he told her, as if explaining something to a child.

'Then you're talking nonsense,' she managed. 'I can love CJ and stay independent? I don't think so.'

'That's what I mean,' he said wearily. 'You're caught. If anything happened to CJ, you'd break your heart, and why put yourself there?' His eyes grew bleak and distant. 'Of all the stupid, irresponsible acts. Stuffing up birth control. Us! Two doctors. We should never have messed up like that. For me to have put you through that…'

And that was the limit. Her anger had boiled straight over to full-blown fury, a fury mixed with desolation, rejection and loss.

She stared at him for a long, baffled minute—and then she reached out and hit him.

A wave caught her just as she did, knocking her sideways into the surf. She'd hit his face but her slap had been deflected, much of its force lost. But she no longer cared. She lay where she'd been knocked, letting the water wash over her, thinking about not even bothering to surface, and when Cal's hand reached down to grab her and haul her up she reacted as if his touch burned.

She kicked out, a futile act in three feet of water, smacked his hands away from her and backed out of the waves. Dumb, useless tears were mixing with the salt water.

'You low-life! Get away from me.'

'Hell, Gina, I didn't mean to say…' Cal sounded horrified.

'You did say,' she spluttered, backing further away from

him. 'Get lost, Cal Jamieson. You say you loved me. That's ridiculous. You don't know the meaning of the word. Leave me be. I'm going back to the hospital. I'm going to check on our baby in the morning and the minute he doesn't need me I'm out of here. I'm out of your life. I'll send you a photo of CJ every year on his birthday. I'm sure that's all you want, Cal Jamieson, and it's all you deserve. Get lost.'

Three hundred miles away another drama was being played out. Another consequence of loving.

'Megan?'

'Go away.' The girl's voice dragged as though there was no strength left in it and her mother's surge of fear grew even stronger. What was happening?

Honey had hoped this day could be different. When she'd persuaded her husband and daughter to go to the rodeo she'd almost allowed herself to be optimistic. She'd hoped it could be time out from the depression that draped this sad old farm-house and the people in it.

But Megan had been silent and sullen all the way to the rodeo, and as soon as they'd arrived she'd disappeared to be by herself in the bush. Well, what was new? Honey had won-dered sadly. For the last few months Megan had glumped round the house in her oversized men's clothes, she'd worked in sullen silence, she'd eaten like there was no stopping her, not caring care how much weight she put on...

Honey Cooper had been concerned about her nineteen-year-old daughter for months, but then she'd also been terri-fied about her husband's failing health. More. She'd been terrified that the bank would finally foreclose on the farm. She'd been terrified that Jim would kill himself. There was only so much terror one woman could hold, and Megan's de-pression had seemed the least of it.

But today there'd been something new. Worse. On the way

home from the rodeo Megan had huddled into the back of the car like a wounded animal. She'd stayed there until Honey had got Jim inside and then Megan had scuttled into her bedroom and locked the door behind her.

Now she'd been in the bathroom for an hour and as Honey had lain beside Jim she'd heard searing, racking sobs that had terrified her past all the rest.

And things she'd been trying hard to ignore had suddenly refused to be ignored a moment longer.

'What the hell's going on with Megan?' Jim asked, and she laid a hand on her husband's arm to stop him getting up. His heart was so bad. He mustn't get upset.

'Hush. I'll go and see.'

'It's not that boy?' Jim rolled over in the dark and stared bleakly at his wife in the moonlight streaming in through the dust-streaked window. 'He wasn't at the rodeo, was he? If he's been seeing her again... If he's hurt her...'

'I'm sure he wasn't there,' Honey said soothingly. 'You know Megan promised she wouldn't see him again. I'm sure she meant it and I'm sure he hasn't tried to see her. Hush. I'll go and see what's wrong.'

But now she stood outside the locked bathroom door and she knew that there was no quick fix available here. Megan's sobs were truly frightening. Megan, who'd held the family together. She'd leaned on her far too much, Honey thought as she asked again that her daughter unlock the door. But what choice did she have?

Megan was nineteen and clever and she'd ached to go to university—but if she'd gone then the hard work here would have killed Jim. So Honey had pressured her to stay. Megan had worked and worked, even after that boy...

'Megan, love, you need to unlock the door.'

'I'm fine.' The words were spoken on a hiccuping sob. 'Go away. I'm fine.'

'*You're not fine and I'm not going away until you open the door. Please, Megan. Your father's worried.*'

Your father's worried. Your father's sick. Your father needs you. Here it was again, Honey thought. Emotional blackmail. But it was all she had.

And it worked now as it had worked before. There was a ragged gasp, a scuffle—sounds of cleaning up?—and then the door was opened a crack.

'*I'm fine,*' Megan said again, harshly into the stillness of the darkened house. '*Tell Dad he doesn't have to worry.*'

'*Come into your room and we'll talk about it.*' She was still whispering. Jim mustn't hear.

'*Why?*' Megan whispered back, just as fiercely. '*There's nothing to talk about.*'

She turned, and as she did, Honey gasped.

Megan was wearing a faded chenille dressing-gown, the sort of shapeless garment she'd been wearing for months. But as she turned against the moonlight streaming in from the window at the end of the passage, Honey had caught her profile.

For months she'd been looking at that profile, thinking no, surely not, that would be the one thing that would kill Jim, please no. It was just weight gain. Megan had been overeating. It had to be the reason.

And now...

'*Oh, God, you've lost it,*' she whispered. '*Meg, you've lost the baby.*'

'*What baby?*'

'*You were pregnant.*'

'*So what?*' Megan said wearily, and Honey grabbed her shoulders and propelled her back into her room and shut the door behind her.

'*You really were.*'

'*Yeah, but I'm not any more.*' The girl's voice sounded exhausted. Defeated.

'What…what happened?'

'It was dead,' Megan whispered, still in that awful, inhuman voice. 'It came early and it was dead. A miscarriage. I miscarried a baby and now it's over. So you don't have to worry. I'm fine.'

'Oh, my dear…' Honey reached out to hug her daughter but Megan flinched away.

'Leave me alone,' she said dully. 'Go back to Dad. Tell him there's no need to worry. I'll go on being his good little girl and he doesn't have to have a heart attack.'

'Megan, that's not fair.'

'My baby's dead,' Megan flashed at her. 'Is that fair?' Then she crumpled back onto the bed, sinking her face into her hands. 'Nothing's fair. The whole world isn't fair.'

'I'll take you to the hospital,' Honey said uncertainly, and Megan's hands dropped from her face so she could stare at her mother in fury.

'You think I shut up for all these months for you to tell Dad now?' she snapped. 'Protect Dad at all costs? Well, I have and there's nothing to do now but go to bed and forget about it.'

'You'll need to be checked.'

'I'm fine.'

'Love…'

'I'm not going anywhere,' Megan whispered. 'I'm not doing anything. You tell anyone and I'll deny it absolutely. The whole thing is over, Mum. Go back to bed.'

She sat, rigid and unmoving, waiting for Honey to leave. Waiting to be alone again. Waiting.

Honey was left with nothing to do. With nowhere to go.

She stared down at her daughter for a long, long minute and Megan glared back, unflinching.

'The baby's dead and it's over,' she whispered. 'There's an end to it. An end to everything.'

'Oh, my love…'

'There's no love about it,' Megan said bleakly. 'Leave me be.'

'Honey?'

It was Jim's voice calling from down the hall, and with a last desperate glance at her daughter Honey turned away.

Megan flinched again.

But she sat unmoving. Then, as the door finally closed behind her mother, the girl hauled herself under the covers—and she started to shake.

CHAPTER SIX

IT WAS almost noon when Gina woke and for a moment she didn't have a clue where she was or what was happening.

Then remembrance flooded back and with it horror.

The events of the day before were a jumbled kaleidoscope of surging emotion. A desperately ill baby. Dead children. Appalling injuries. Cal…

CJ. She reached out and his warm little body wasn't beside her. Of course. He was with the Grubbs.

Still?

She checked her watch and gasped. What was she thinking of, sleeping this late? The baby, CJ—she'd have been needed and no one had called. She threw back her covers and then gasped again as a man's silhouette blocked the sun.

'You might like to reconsider getting out of bed,' Cal drawled. 'Unless you're wearing more than it looks like you're wearing from out here.'

He was on the veranda. She'd left the door open last night to let in the sea breeze, and he was blocking the doorway. And as for what she was wearing… Last night—or early this morning—she'd simply stripped off her sea-soaked clothes, stood under a cold shower until her burning body had cooled and then fallen straight into bed.

And now here was Cal, right in the doorway.

'Go away,' she snapped, and hauled her sheet up to her chin.

'I brought you your luggage,' he told her, not going away at all but walking into her room and dumping her gear at the foot of the bed. 'You could at least sound grateful.'

'I'm grateful,' she told him, glaring enough to give the lie to her words. But then she looked at the single red bag he was carrying and was distracted enough to be deflected. 'I had two bags. A red and a green one.'

'The red one's heavy enough.'

'I had a small green one.'

'It didn't come back, then,' he told her. 'The coach-line people delivered one red bag this morning but that was all there was. Problem?'

She caught herself. 'Um…no.' No problem. She was staying next door to a hospital after all.

Right. Where was she? Glaring.

'There's no problem if you go away,' she told him, and he had the temerity to smile.

'OK. But I've also brought you your son.'

CJ. She sat up, cautiously, still holding her sheet. 'What have you done with CJ?'

'You sound as if you expect that I've corrupted him by just existing.'

'Don't be ridiculous,' she told him, still trying to hold her glower. Drat the man, why did he have to smile like that? 'Where is he?'

'He was right behind me but his puppy escaped into the garden. I can see them from here. The puppy seems to be investigating the lorikeets in the grevillea and CJ is supervising.'

She tried to sort this information but found it even more confusing. 'His puppy?'

'The Grubbs have given your son…our son…a puppy.'

There was a lot in that statement to consider—so she stuck to the easiest bit. 'CJ can't have a puppy,' she said blankly.

'I would have thought that.' Cal stood at the end of her bed and looked at her, speculation and amusement lurking in those deep eyes. 'But you did leave him with the Grubbs for the night.'

'I didn't mean to.'

'No, but you did, and the Grubbs are warm-hearted people who maybe lack a little in the grey-matter department. They have a puppy they don't want—their bitch has a habit of finding all sorts of unsuitable partners and the Grubb puppies are legion in this place—and they've seen a little boy who falls in love. So they've done the obvious thing.'

Still too much information. She couldn't figure it all out. And why was he standing there, just…smiling?

'We're going back to the States,' she told him.

'I guess the puppy is, too, then.'

'Oh, for heaven's sake.' She went to toss back the covers, remembered and grabbed them back again. 'Go away so I can dress.'

'I'll wait on the veranda.'

'Wait anywhere you like. Just not here.'

'I'll watch CJ, shall I?'

'Watch him all you want.'

'Gina…'

'Yes?'

'You're not being very kind.'

'Why should I be kind?' she demanded. 'Just go away, Cal Jamieson. You don't make me feel kind at all.'

By the time she'd showered and dressed she'd simmered down a little—but not much. Not enough. She walked out onto the veranda wearing her own clothes, a soft linen skirt and a T-shirt that didn't look businesslike but at least made her feel clean and normal and almost in charge of her world. It was great to have her own gear. Or almost all her own gear. Then she saw Cal with her son and she forgot about her luggage and she wasn't in charge of her world any more at all.

They were so alike it was breathtaking. Heartbreaking.

From the time CJ had been born she'd seen Cal every time she'd looked into her son's face, and now, seeing them side by side, it was almost too much for her. When she walked out onto the veranda CJ was wearing Bruce's hat, but the pup bounced up and knocked it off. Cal retrieved it and together they carefully inspected it for damage. CJ's wiry curls, the intent look in his eyes, the way his forehead puckered in concentration… Their heads were almost touching, the sound of Cal's grave voice telling the pup to leave the hat alone, CJ's higher voice raised in a copied command—and then a low chuckle and a high-pitched giggle as the puppy bounced up and raced off with the hat again…

Practicalities, she told herself fiercely as she dug her hands deep into her skirt's side pockets and walked steadily down the steps to meet them.

They heard her sandals on the steps and Cal turned—but as he turned, the pup saw a new pair of legs coming toward him, dropped the hat and bounced over to investigate.

For the first time she focussed on the dog. What was it?

A cross between a Dalmatian and a boxer with a bit of cocker spaniel thrown in, she thought. It looked half-grown, long and gangly and all legs. White with black spots. A face that looked like it had just been punched flat. Great ears that dangled past his collar.

He reached her and jumped up, his large paws landing on her thigh and darned near knocking her over. He looked up at her, and she could swear his big stupid canine face was grinning, and his black and white tail was wagging so fast it could have made electricity.

'What sort of a dog is this?' she gasped, trying to back off. But the pup wasn't having any of it. He was leaping up and dancing around her, barking and grinning and grinning, and despite herself she had to grin back.

'His name is Rudolph, after a ballet dancer Mrs Grubb saw on TV,' CJ told her, looking at his mother with a certain amount of anxiety. 'Mrs Grubb says he's going to be the best dog in the world and he prances just like a ballet dancer. Can we keep him?'

Rudolph had raced back down to his new would-be owner. Now he squatted in pounce position, leapt at CJ, knocked him down, licked his face, then galloped back to Gina. Gina backed fast but he jumped up, the backs of her legs caught the veranda steps and she sat down. Hard.

Rudolph licked with a tongue that was roughly the size of a large facecloth.

'Ugh,' Gina said, stunned. She wiped her face and watched the dog gallop over to Cal.

'Sit,' Cal said.

Rudolph sat.

The tail was going ballistic.

'CJ, we can't keep this dog,' she said, and if her voice sounded desperate, who could blame her? 'For a start there's no way we can take him home. He can hardly sit on my lap on the plane.'

'He can sit on mine,' CJ said stoutly, and Cal choked.

'You laugh and I'm going to have to kill you,' Gina said conversationally, and focussed on CJ. Or tried to focus on CJ. 'I'm sorry about last night,' she told him. 'Did you mind sleeping at Mrs Grubb's?'

'No, because of Rudolph,' he told her. 'Mom, Mr Grubb says he has to take a dead tree to the rubbish tip and I can go in his truck if I want, and Rudolph can come, too, but I have to ask you first so Cal said we should wake you up.'

'Gee, thanks, Cal,' she said, and glowered.

'Think nothing of it,' Cal said, smiling blandly. 'But Mr Grubb's waiting. Can CJ go? Grubb's very reliable.'

There were three faces looking at her in mute appeal.
CJ's, Cal's, Rudolph's. She was so out of her depth she was
drowning.

'Fine,' she told them all, and was rewarded by a war whoop
and the sight of her small son—and dog—flying away across
the lawn to the dubious attractions of Crocodile Creek's rubbish tip.

'I haven't even thought about when we're leaving,' Gina
said, staring after her son in dismay.

'Good,' Cal told her.

'You're not still on about Townsville?' she snapped, and
he had the grace to look a bit shamefaced.

'No. Gina, I'm sorry about last night.'

'Good.'

'I pushed you for my own ends.'

'So you did.'

'And I never meant that I didn't want CJ to have been
born. Of course I didn't.'

'Fine.' She glowered. It seemed to be becoming a perma-
nent state.

'But it would be good for CJ to be raised where I could
have some access.'

'So move to the States.'

'My base is here.'

'No,' she said, and her anger faded a bit as she turned to
face him square on. 'You don't have a base.'

'I've been here for four years.'

'Yes, but you don't love anyone here.'

'That's irrelevant.'

'No, it's not.'

'Gina…'

'You don't need any of these people,' she said. She'd gone
to bed last night thinking of Cal, thinking of what was happening with him, and this discussion seemed an extension of

that. It might be intrusive—none of her business—but him pushing her last night seemed to have removed the barriers to telling things how they were. 'Cal, you're spending your whole life patching people up, picking up the pieces, in medicine and in your personal life. Like with me. I came out here five years ago desperately unhappy and you picked up the pieces and you patched me up and I fell deeply in love with you. But then you don't take the next step. You never admit you need anyone else. Is there anyone here you need? Really, Cal?'

'I…'

'Of course there's not,' she said, almost cordially. 'Because of what happened with your family, you've never let yourself need anyone again.'

'What is this?' he demanded, startled. 'Psychology by Dr Lopez?'

'I know. It's none of my business,' she told him, gentling. 'But it's why I have to go home. Because I've admitted that I need people. I need my family and my friends.' More, she thought, and the idea that swept across her heart was so strong that she knew it for absolute truth. She needed Cal. But she wouldn't say that. She'd said it years ago, and where had that got her?

'For me to calmly go and live in Townsville would hurt,' she told him. 'Sure, I'd have a great job…'

'You'd meet people.'

'So I would,' she told him. 'But not the people I love.'

'You'd learn…'

'You really don't understand the need thing, do you, Cal?' she said sadly. 'I need my friends and I need my family and I'm not too scared to admit it.'

'You're saying I am?'

'I'm not saying anything,' she said wearily. 'But Townsville's not going to happen.' She regrouped. Sort of. 'And Rudolph's not going to happen either,' she told him, 'so stop encouraging CJ.'

'I'm not.'

'Just stop it,' she said. She closed her eyes for a moment, still trying for the regroup. 'The baby. Lucky. How is he?'

'He's still holding his own,' Cal told her. They'd both moved back into the shade of the veranda—in this climate you moved into the shade as if a magnet was pulling you. 'There doesn't seem any sign of infection. His heartbeat's settling and steady.'

'I'll do another echocardiogram now.'

'We thought you'd say that, so we waited for you to wake up.'

'You should have—'

'There was no need,' he said gently, and she flushed. She hated it when he was gentle. She hated it when he was…how she loved him. 'What about the bleeding?'

'The results of yesterday's blood tests should be in soon,' he told her. 'Alix, our pathologist, is working on them now.'

'I haven't used any clot-breaking medication,' she said. 'Usually after a procedure for pulmonary stenosis I'd prescribe a blood thinner but I've held off. There's a fair risk of blood clots in infants this tiny, but if he's a bleeder…'

'Hamish concurs,' he told her. 'He's saying von Willebrand's is a strong possibility.'

She nodded, flinching inside as she thought through the consequences.

Von Willebrand's was a treatable condition. A similar disorder to haemophilia, any cut or major bruising could be life-threatening, but treated it was far less dangerous. In fact, given this baby's condition, it was a bonus in that it made it less likely that Lucky would get a clot.

But it left an even deeper sense of unease about the mother. A woman, or more likely a girl, who'd had no medical help during a birth, who had possibly told no one about the birth, who was on her own.

Was she right in her surmise that the girl wasn't a bleeder? If she'd haemorrhaged afterwards...

'Has there been any news about the mother?'

'Nothing,' Cal told her, and she could see by his face that he was following her train of thought and was as worried as she was. 'The police and a couple of local trackers have been right through the bushland round the rodeo area. They're sure that she's no longer in the area. She must have come by car and left by car.'

'Or by bus.'

'Or bus.'

'And maybe she has von Willebrand's disease. Maybe she's a bleeder.'

'She or the father,' Cal said.

'I'm not worrying about the father right now,' Gina told him. 'I'm worrying too much about the mother. To give birth in such a place, to leave thinking your baby was dead... What she must be going through.'

They fell silent. Each knew what the other was thinking. Suicide was a very real possibility. If only they knew where she was. Who she was.

'There's no matching prenatal mothers in our records at all,' Cal told her. 'No clues.'

'I thought everyone knew everyone in this district.'

'No one knows who this is.'

'Someone must,' Gina said, and Cal nodded.

More silence.

'Charles says his father had von Willebrand's,' Cal said, and Gina frowned.

'Charles?'

'Our medical director. The guy in the wheelchair.'

'I know who Charles is,' she snapped. 'Charles's father has von Willebrand's?'

'Had. He's dead.'

'Charles is a local?' Gina was still thinking it through. 'Von Willebrand's is a rare blood disorder. In such a small community there has to be some connection.'

'We talked it through last night,' Cal told her. 'After you and I…' He broke off. 'Well, when I came back to the house Charles was still awake and we ended up talking things through till almost dawn. Like you, when he said that I thought there must be a connection. But it seems unlikely.'

'Why? Tell me about his family.'

'Charles is a Wetherby. The Wetherbys own one of the biggest stations in the state—Wetherby Downs. Charles's brother runs the station now.' Cal hesitated. 'I'm not sure why, but Charles and his family don't get on. Charles was hurt in a shooting accident when he was eighteen. He went to the city for medical treatment, ended up staying to do medicine and only came back here to set up this service. He hasn't had much to do with his family for years. But as for the von Willebrand's…. Charles himself doesn't have kids. His brother doesn't have von Willebrand's, and his brother's two kids are only fourteen and sixteen.'

'The sixteen-year-old?' she said quickly. 'That'd fit. A girl?

'Yes, but—'

'A teenager in trouble and desperate not to tell her parents?'

'Charles checked it out this morning,' Cal told her. 'She's in boarding school in Sydney and hasn't been home for a month.'

'So we'll cross her off the list,' Gina said reluctantly. 'Is there no other family?'

'Charles's only other sibling is a sister who moved to Sydney over twenty years back,' he told her. 'It was a lead worth following but it's going nowhere.'

'It just seems such a coincidence,' she murmured. 'It's so rare.'

'Charles's father was not exactly a man of honour,' Cal told her. 'Charles volunteered that last night. The man was filthy rich, and used to get what he wanted. There's more than an odds-on chance that he played around.'

'But he's dead,' Gina said. 'So we can't ask him if he fathered anyone who might or might not have fathered someone who's just had a baby. We're clutching at straws here.' She sighed. 'OK. Enough. I'll go and see the baby now.' She hesitated. 'But last night… The accident, the repercussions…'

'Will be felt throughout the district for ever,' Cal told her heavily. 'I'm going out to the aboriginal settlement later this afternoon.'

'Do you want me to come with you?' Now, where had that come from? She hadn't meant to offer. It had just slipped out.

'I'd like that,' he said gravely, and she cast him a sideways look of suspicion.

'Maybe I shouldn't.'

'Gina, you would help,' he told her. 'You're good with people. You know what to say.'

'So do you,' she said bitterly. 'The Dr Jamieson specialty. Picking up the pieces.' She shook her head. 'Sorry. I'm not going there any more. But I will come to the settlement with you. I might as well be useful now I'm here. OK, Dr Jamieson. Let's move on.'

Cal had patients booked to see him. He had to leave her—for which Gina was profoundly grateful. Sort of. With CJ happily carting junk and Cal disappearing, she was left on her own.

She spent a few minutes calming down and then went to find a pharmacist.

She wanted to see the baby but she had priorities of her own first.

The hospital dispensary was deserted. Open at need, she

thought, and tried to figure who to ask. Not Cal. But as she turned away Charles was behind her in his wheelchair and she jumped almost a foot.

'Do you mind?' she asked breathlessly, and he grinned.

'Sorry. I've tried to get a wheelchair that does footsteps but they don't make them.'

'I'm sorry.'

'Don't be. My speciality's scaring people. And I'm sorry about last night. Talk about throwing you in at the deep end…'

'It was awful,' she admitted. 'But maybe less awful for me who doesn't know the people and who won't be round to cope with the consequences.'

'Cal reminded me you used to run a kids' group at Townsville.'

'So I did,' she told him.

'You don't fancy doing it again?' he asked mildly. 'There's a screaming need here.'

'Cal suggested that,' she told him. 'But he suggested I do it at Townsville.'

Charles's face stilled. He looked at her for a long minute and then he grimaced.

'Cal's a fool.'

'No.' She shrugged. 'Not a fool. And I'm going home. There's no place here for me.'

'There's always a place here for you,' Charles told her forcibly. 'Your reputation from Townsville was that of a splendid doctor and we'd be honoured to have you stay. Apart from really, really needing a cardiologist.'

'And where does that leave Cal?'

'Having to face what he should have faced five years ago,' Charles told her.

She shook her head and closed her eyes. 'Leave it, Charles.'

He looked up at her for a long minute—and then he sighed.

'OK, We'll leave it.' He glanced up at her face once more

and then through to the empty dispensary. 'Were you looking for something?'

'A pharmacist.'

'We don't have such a thing. We get what we need when we need it. Do you need something?'

'Insulin.'

There was an even longer pause. 'For you?' he asked at last, and Gina thought, Yes, the man was fast. He'd have figured it couldn't have been for CJ. She'd never have been able to leave him with strangers if it had been CJ.

'Yes. For me.'

He frowned. 'Does Cal know you're diabetic?'

'Cal doesn't know the first thing about me,' she told him. 'But that's irrelevant. I had my main supply of insulin in my second suitcase, which still seems to be lost. I carry enough for two or three days in my hand luggage but I'll be needing more by tomorrow.'

'I'll organise it for you,' he told her. 'Is there anything else you need?'

'An air ticket home?'

'I'll organise that, too,' he told her, but then he hesitated. 'Gina, can you give us another forty-eight hours? I'd like to have Lucky really out of the woods before you go.'

'With Hamish and Emily, you hardly need me.'

'I know I hardly need you,' he growled. 'But it's the *hardly* I don't like. I don't want to lose this kid. And neither do you.'

'No.'

'So you'll stay two more days?'

'I guess.' There was a lot to be sorted, she thought. She had to come to some arrangement with Cal by then. She had to figure out what sort of father he was prepared to be.

Then there was the added complication of Rudolph.

She sighed.

'I do need another couple of nights,' she told him.

'A couple of years would be good.'

'Don't push it.'

Next on her list was Lucky. Gina walked into the nursery and found not one but two doctors clucking over him. Hamish was checking a drip and Em was consulting patient notes, but both of them looked up with such guilty starts as she walked in that she smiled.

'Don't tell me. Both of you should be somewhere else.'

'We're just looking,' Hamish told her, and smiled. His smile was a bit forced, though, and Gina knew exactly what was happening. After a night like last night, there was a huge need for at least one happy ending and she had a feeling that she wasn't the only one to have an urge to hug. Babies were excellent therapy. As if he was reading her thoughts, Hamish continued. 'You've just missed Cal.'

'And Charles before him,' Emily said ruefully. 'Anyone who's anyone has been in to check on our little Lucky this morning.' She moved aside. 'Now it's your turn. Go right ahead. Do your checking.'

She did.

He looked different today, Gina thought. A little…fuller? Yesterday he'd been barely alive. Now, even though he was still a tiny scrap of crumpled babyhood, Lucky's eyes were wide, his tiny fists were flailing, and she had the strongest urge to pick him up and gather him to her.

She couldn't. Hamish had him wired for everything—the technology surrounding this baby was far, far bulkier than the baby himself. It almost seemed ridiculous. So much technology on something so small.

Her hands slid into the incubator port and she stroked the little one's cheek, and then she slid her little finger into the palm of the tiny hand. His fingers curled around and held, and Gina had to fight back a sudden, stupid surge of tears.

'You don't need me here,' she said blindly, gently releasing her finger and starting to turn away.

But Hamish caught her shoulder and turned her back.

'We do need you, Gina,' he said softly. 'You did a wonderful job here. I've only read of the operation you did on Lucky yesterday. I haven't even seen it. I rang the paediatric cardiologist in Sydney this morning and he's stunned it's gone so well.'

'That's…good. I was lucky.'

'Lucky was lucky,' Hamish told her, and smiled. 'And last night we were lucky to have you again. And Cal… Cal's lucky that he met you.'

'We think he loves you,' Emily said, and Gina blinked.

'Um…excuse me?'

'He's been faithful for years.'

'Sure.'

'He has.'

'Because I'm an excuse.'

'Yes, but you're more than an excuse,' Emily told her. 'He really fell hard. Charles said—'

'You've all been talking about me.'

'It's the doctors' house,' Hamish said, as if that explained everything. 'We all talk about everyone. And we worry about Cal.'

'He's big enough to worry about himself.'

'But if he had a son—' Em started, but Gina had had enough.

'Look, leave it,' she said, more roughly than she'd intended, but Hamish looked at Emily as if for confirmation and then went in anyway.

'Gina, you fought for Lucky,' he said gently. 'Emily and Charles and I think you should fight for Cal. He's worth fighting for.'

'I've been fighting for years,' she said bitterly. 'I'm past fighting.'

'But Cal—'

'Sure, Cal's had it hard,' she snapped. 'But I haven't exactly had it easy. I've been fighting for my husband's life, for my son's welfare and for my own health.' She caught herself and bit her lip, angry with herself more than them. These were Cal's friends. Sure, they were interfering more than she liked—a lot more than she liked—but she wasn't in familiar territory and what she should do now was back out.

So she backed out. Fast. Letting her eyes drop again to Lucky as she did.

He was so perfect.

'I'm going out to the settlement with Cal,' she said, and Emily smiled.

'That's great.'

'It's not great. But…keep Lucky safe for me while I'm away.'

'We will, that,' Hamish told her softly. 'Of course we will. And in return, can we ask that you keep an open mind?'

'An open mind and an open heart?' she demanded, meeting his look head on. 'Is that what you mean? If it is, I tried that five years ago and it didn't work. What makes you think it'll work now?'

Megan woke and for a moment she'd forgotten. She lay in her sweat-soaked bed and let herself stay blank. Just for a moment.

But then her mother was there, holding her hand, sitting on the bed, terror flooding her face.

'Dad,' Megan whispered. She was accustomed to that terror. 'Something's happened to Dad.'

But it seemed that the terror had been redirected. The terror was for her.

'Sweetheart, we need to get you to a doctor,' Honey was saying, and yesterday flooded back in all its horror. Megan cringed.

'No.'

'You're ill. You're soaking in sweat.'

'I'll get over it.'

'Megan, you must let me take you—'

'There's no must about it,' Megan told her, fighting for strength to sound sure. 'OK, I'm ill, but I'll get recover. Tell Dad I've got the flu. Don't let him near me. Tell him he'll catch it. I'm sorry, Mum, but you'll have to do my chores…'

'Oh, sweetheart…'

'Just for a day or two,' Megan mumbled. The effort she'd made saying just those words had been too much for her and she was wilting. 'But you don't want to tell Dad anything else. Do you?'

'Of course I don't.'

'There you go, then,' Megan said wearily. To tell Jim was unthinkable. Protect him at all costs. 'Leave it. Leave me be. I'll be just…fine.'

CHAPTER SEVEN

WHY had she said she'd go out to the settlement with Cal? She must have been mad. But after a couple of hours of staying back at the doctors' residence, watching CJ play with a pup he couldn't keep, seeing every other doctors' eyes on her, staying started to seem a pretty bleak alternative.

After the chaos of yesterday the hospital was quiet. Gina had thought she'd be needed for Lucky but Emily had been hovering over the little one, almost possessive. 'Emily's had a bad time lately,' Charles told her. 'She needs distraction and if that distraction's the baby then we'll let her be.'

This hospital was more of a family than a medical clinic, Gina thought, and Charles's speculative gaze on her made her feel intensely uncomfortable. Who knew what he was deciding that she needed?

She'd offered to help with the kids from the night before, but she was stymied there as well.

'The worst of the cases are being transferred to Cairns,' Charles told her.

There was another pang as Gina saw the plane take off. She should be on it.

'But you've offered to go out to the settlement with Cal,' Charles said.

'I could change my mind.'

'Cal needs you.'

'He doesn't need anyone,' she snapped, but Charles just smiled his wry smile and told her that in a medical capacity she'd be useful and he'd be delighted if she stayed. As she'd agreed to.

So she agreed. She'd run out of excuses. CJ and Walter Grubb had decided they were friends for life and there was more trash to cart. There was nothing for it but to decide this afternoon was just something to be worked through.

But it was hard. She sat beside Cal as the miles disappeared under their wheels and thought she'd been mad. She tried to think of something to say and nothing came.

Silence. Cal's face was set and grim.

Silence, silence and more silence.

Then, out of nowhere, Cal snapped 'How long have you been diabetic?'

It was almost an explosion. His knuckles were white on the steering-wheel and she stared at him in astonishment.

'How did you know?'

'Charles told me. Just now. He asked me how long you'd been diabetic, whether you were type one or two, how your control was—and you know what? I didn't even know you were diabetic. You couldn't have been one five years ago. Were you?'

He wanted her to say no, Gina thought. He sounded almost desperate.

'I've been diabetic since I was twelve,' she told him. 'Type one.'

'You weren't diabetic when you were here.'

'Of course I was.'

'You were living with me,' he said explosively. 'Sharing my bed. Sharing my life. How can I have not known you were diabetic?'

'No,' she said softly. 'You weren't sharing my life. We were lovers, Cal. We hadn't taken it further.'

'We were living together.'

'Cal, if we'd been really living together—really sharing our lives—do you think I could have kept something like that from you?'

'You must have hidden—'

'I hid nothing,' she said wearily. 'But you were so contained. I was hopelessly in love with you but you never shared your life. I had to drag your family history from you. You'd come home after a dreadful day—after some trauma or other—and you'd take my body as if you were desperate, but you'd never talk to me about what you were feeling. And me... You saw what you wanted to see, Cal. I remember at the end, when I was just starting to suspect I was pregnant. I was feeling ghastly and my blood sugars were all over the place and I was desperate. You came home that last night we had together and said I looked pale and what was wrong, and I told you I'd had a tummy bug. "Do you need medication?" you asked. When I said no, you hugged me and told me to go to bed and you considerately didn't touch me for the rest of the night. When I was crying out to be touched. Then next morning you asked if I was fine, and you believed me and went off to your urgent medical call. Even though I was shaky and white-faced and sick. Because you wanted me to be fine. You wanted me to slot into the edges of your life—the parts that were available.'

'But you're diabetic,' he said, sounding confused but also exasperated. 'Why hide it?'

'Because that would have made me way too needy,' she said, knowing that he wouldn't understand but not being able to think of any other way of explaining.

'Needy...'

'I was already in need,' she told him. 'I came to Townsville after Paul had asked for a separation and I was a mess. And you picked me up and put the pieces back together. Then... then you couldn't figure out where to go from there.'

'I don't know what you mean.'

'I don't suppose you do,' she said sadly. 'Because what I needed was for you to need me, and that was never going to happen. It was so one-sided. You fell for me because I leaned on you, and as soon as I didn't need you in a way you understood then you got uncomfortable. I sensed as much really early. I thought that I'd been stupid in the first place, letting myself lean on you, and if you knew I was diabetic then you'd figure I needed you still more, and the relationship would never go past being you the rescuer.'

'This isn't making sense.'

'It's not, is it?' she said. 'But I hate people feeling sorry for me because I'm diabetic.'

'I wouldn't have felt sorry for you.'

'No, but you would have supported me, and it would have felt more as if I needed you, and there was no way our relationship was going to work out that way. I was fighting so hard to get through to you on a personal level. And then I got pregnant and Paul was injured and it didn't matter any more anyway.'

He shook his head, obviously still trying to work things out.

'Your diabetes,' he said at last, and she Gina knew he was returning to medicine because that was an easy route. When in emotional crisis, turn to what you're good at.

Well, why not? 'What about my diabetes?'

'It's obviously well controlled.'

'Why obviously?'

'Because I never knew.' Once again he seemed to be fighting to contain anger.

'It wasn't, actually,' she told him. 'I've struggled for years and my pregnancy was a nightmare. But there's a new background insulin that was released last year and it's fabulous. I haven't had a hypo since I've been on it.'

'You never had a hypo when you were with me.'

'Of course I did.'

'When?'

'It mostly happened at night,' she told him. 'I'd wake feeling dizzy and sick and I'd head to the kitchen for juice. I did my injecting in the bathroom.'

'I never heard.'

'Of course you didn't.'

'What's that supposed to mean?'

'After we'd made love,' she said softly, remembering, 'you'd sleep on the far side of the bed so I didn't disturb you. You needed space, as I remember. You always needed space.'

More silence. Loaded silence.

'I'd have seen your injecting sites,' he said at last.

'Would you?' She shrugged. 'That needs real intimacy, Cal. Making love in the daylight with our eyes open. We hadn't reached it. I'm not sure we would have.'

'Why are you telling me this now?'

'I'm being honest. I don't know where else to go.'

'You don't need to go anywhere.'

'Meaning what?'

'Meaning you have to stay here.' The anger was growing, she thought, and the anger was self-directed. Fury at himself for not noticing?

Just plain fury.

'You can't go back to the States,' he told her.

'Why on earth not?'

'Hell, Gina, you need—'

'I don't need anything,' she flashed at him. 'Get that through your head, will you? I don't need you. CJ doesn't need a father. He's got great memories of Paul and they'll last him a lifetime. I don't need a husband. I have family and friends back in Idaho. I have a great career. I'm not a lost soul here, Cal.'

'I can look after you.' It was as if he wasn't hearing her. He was gripping the steering-wheel so tightly it was likely to crack at any minute.

'I can look after myself.'

'Look, Townsville was a bad idea,' he said. 'I know that. It was a dumb suggestion. At least, by yourself it was a bad idea. But together maybe things could work as they did last time you were here. We could set up house here.'

'You're not suggesting I marry you?' she said, astounded.

'We're good together.'

'No, we're not. Have you been listening to a thing I've been saying?'

'How did you cope with a pregnancy and type one diabetes and a quadriplegic husband?' he demanded, and she sighed.

'I'm sure I don't know. And I did it without you. Astounding, isn't it?'

'It's not astounding,' he said, catching the sarcasm in her voice and his own voice gentling in response. 'But it must have been hell.'

'Maybe. But that's got nothing to do with the here and now. Or with what I do in the future.'

'You say you love me.'

'That has nothing to do with it either,' she told him.

'Hell, Gina, if I'd known… If you knew how much I'd wondered about you…'

'You would have come galloping to the rescue,' she whispered.

'Of course I would. Gina, I love you.'

'See, that's the problem here.' She bit her lip, aware that her hold on the thread of this conversation was growing tenuous. She was barely making sense to herself, much less to him. 'I'm not sure you've really figured that out. You think it was dumb not telling you I was diabetic. You don't know why I didn't tell you.'

'No, but—'

'Shut up, Cal,' she told him. 'Just shut up.'

The country around the car was changing now, the bush-land near the coast giving way to the rocky country where they'd driven last night. They were nearing the site of the crash. Cal slowed, but there was no need. There were a couple of deep gashes in the gravel, a pool of spilt oil but nothing else. Everything had been cleared.

They drove in silence for a couple of minutes more, and Gina knew Cal was thinking exactly what she was thinking. What an appalling waste. And how quickly life could be snuffed out.

Was she crazy, throwing away Cal's offer? she wondered. He was saying marry him. Live here. Happily ever after?

Maybe she was just plain dumb, but she glanced across at Cal's set face and knew she was exactly right. She had no choice.

'Cal, I don't want a relationship based on need,' she told him. 'Or…not just my need. Sure, I love you but…'

'Well, then—'

'Let me explain,' she snapped. Honestly. Maybe a letter would be easier. She had to get her tongue around the right words.

'Even if I needed you—which I don't—that's no basis for a marriage,' she told him. 'Paul taught me that. He worked out the hard way that marriage was a really special thing. He sacrificed a lot to try and find it, and he didn't find it for himself, but I know exactly what it is and I'm not prepared to opt for second best. Cal, I love you, and all right, in one sense—in the sense of never being really happy apart—I need you. You say you love me and you want me, but you're only admitting that to yourself because you believe that I need you. You'd never in a pink fit say that you need me.'

'I don't need anyone.'

'There's the rub,' she said sadly. 'There's the reason the whole thing's not going to end in happy ever after. Because you won't let yourself need. You won't cuddle me to comfort yourself because you might get dependent. You say you didn't know I was diabetic? That's because you were so busy preserving your private space that you didn't notice that I had mine. I'm sorry, Cal, but CJ and I need more than that.'

'Gina, I'm asking you to marry me.'

'Am I expected to be grateful?'

'No. Yes. But—'

'I am grateful, Cal,' she said, softening in front of the anguish in his face. 'And I would love to be married to you. But I need to be needed, too, and I won't spend my life being grateful.' She thought about it—or tried to think about it. They were approaching the settlement now and time was running out.

'Cal, I want you to sleep with me and hold me and miss me desperately when I'm not there,' she told him, speaking almost to herself rather than him. 'I don't want you to train yourself to sleep on the other side of the bed in case one day I disappear. I want a relationship that's based on us being together for ever. Sure, one day it'll end and it'll hurt like crazy when that happens, but your way, hurt will be there all the time. Why let that happen when we could have forty years of cuddling?'

She caught her breath and blinked. Whoa, she was being too deep for comfort.

'Unless you snore,' she added, trying frantically to retrieve the situation. 'Then you're off to your side of the bed so fast you'll probably be ejected to the middle of next week.'

He didn't smile He didn't even try to smile.

'Gina, I can't do that,' she said slowly. 'You know I can't. What you're asking…'

'Is too much. I know that. That's why I'm going home.' She took a deep breath and tried to regroup. 'So let's cut out the talk of marriage, Cal Jamieson,' she told him. 'Let's see what this community needs. Move back to medicine. It's the only sanity in a world that seems often to be nuts in every other department. Tomorrow Bruce has asked that CJ and I go croc spotting with him, and the day after that I'm going home. We'll exchange Christmas cards and birthday cards and leave it at that. Your precious independence won't be compromised at all.'

'There has to be a middle road.'

'There isn't,' she said bluntly. 'Get used to it.'

Jim Cooper stood at the back step and watched Honey usher the house cow into the bale. And frowned. Megan did the milking. She'd done the milking since she was eight years old. To see his wife doing it...well, something was wrong.

'What's wrong with Meg?'

'She's not well,' Honey said in a clipped, strained voice that was unusual for the determinedly cheerful Honey.

That was when Jim felt the first shiver of fear. Or maybe it was more than a shiver. Maybe he knew that this was the end.

Honey had lost her optimism.

It was Honey's hopefulness that kept this family together, he thought. No matter what happened, Honey had always said things would be fine.

When the Wetherbys had cut off access to the creek at the crossing, meaning their stock were at the mercy of the district's notoriously unreliable rainfall, Honey had said they'd cope. There wouldn't be a drought. The rains would be reliable, at least until they'd got Megan through university and had saved enough for retirement.

When the drought had hit she'd said they could weather it. They could sell some stock and Megan didn't have to go to university quite yet.

When he'd had his heart attack she'd said it had just been minor, hadn't the doctor said? And, yes, he needed bypass surgery, but if they couldn't afford it then that was that, and surely a minor heart attack meant that the bypass could wait until after the rains came.

Meanwhile she and Megan were strong and they didn't mind doing more than their share of the work.

Then when Megan had fallen in love with that boy, she'd said she'd get over it, she was young, there were lots more boys, but, please, God, she wouldn't find one until after the rains because they needed Megan so much, and wasn't it lucky Megan was such a good girl?

Honey. The eternal optimist. But now... Honey's face was pressed against the cow's warm flank and she looked...defeated.

'What's wrong with Megan?' Jim asked again.

'Women's troubles.'

'Yeah?'

'And maybe she has some sort of infection,' Honey added reluctantly. 'Yeah, that'll be it. Women's troubles and flu. Don't go near her, Jim. I don't want you to catch it.'

Jim stared down at his wife for a long time. Honey kept on with her milking, methodically clearing the teats, her face carefully expressionless.

'I will check Megan,' Jim said at last. 'Sorry, Honey, but you can't protect me from everything for ever.'

The afternoon was a long one.

Cal came out to this settlement once a week. They rotated this duty, so three different doctors visited, with three different specialties. The settlement had a population of two to three hundred but the numbers changed as the various nomadic tribes arrived and stayed for a time before taking off on walkabout again. The nomads were generally healthy, Cal knew. It was those whose tribes had dwindled so far as to make the nomadic lifestyle untenable—those whose backgrounds had hauled them out of the ancient ways and left them with nothing to replace it—they were the ones who were in trouble. They stayed in these camps with no plan for the future, and in many cases they had drifted into despair.

Cal came out here once a week and he worked through medical problems, but every time he came here he tried to figure out how he could help.

Without getting involved.

His first patient for the afternoon was a teenager with a ragged gash from a fight involving broken bottles. His second patient was the kid's opponent. The cuts had been roughly patched but they needed deep cleaning, debridement, an administration of fast-acting antibiotics and a lecture on care.

The lecture would fall on deaf ears.

Five years ago he'd started a club for kids like these back at Townsville. Gina had talked him into it. But after she'd left… He'd gone down to the club and he'd realised that these kids had given him comfort. That helping kids like these had felt good.

That he'd cared.

And the knowledge had had him backing off as if he'd been burned. He'd told himself he needed to move to Crocodile Creek. He needed to concentrate on his medicine, and he couldn't do that if he was emotionally involved.

Work.

'Why the hell,' he asked the boy he was stitching, 'were you fighting with broken bottles? I thought you and Aaron were mates.'

'We were on the petrol,' the boy said, a bit shamefaced. 'I was off me head, like. Aaron was, too. After the accident…all our mates dead…we didn't know what else to do so we started on the petrol to kill time till the olds got back from the hospital. Aaron must'a said something to set me off, but dunno what. Just lucky it hurt, like, before we got too far.'

'Before the community had someone else to mourn,' Cal said grimly. 'Slicing like this could have meant you bled to death.'

'Nah.'

Cal sighed. Petrol sniffing was endemic here, used to alleviate boredom, loneliness, dissociation. There were so many problems.

He looked over to where Gina sat under a stand of eucalypts. She was in the midst of a group of women and their distress was obvious. Karen's grandmother was over there, Cal saw. Mary Wingererra. As he watched, Gina put her arm round the old lady's shoulders and hugged her.

She went in fast and hard, Cal thought. Maybe he should, too.

Could he? She thought he should. Her accusation was that he didn't care. It was unfair. That was the problem. He cared too much.

'When did you last go to school?' he asked Chris, the kid he was stitching, and the thirteen-year-old looked at him as if he was joking.

'School?'

'It's an option.'

'No one goes to school. It's not cool.'

It was the only option, Cal thought. Education was the only way out of this mess.

Yeah, but how…?

It was too hard. Once he'd thought he might try, but then Gina had walked away and he'd abandoned his kids' club when he'd left Townsville. It had hurt like hell and he wasn't putting himself through that again.

Don't get involved. Treat what's hurting and move on.

Gina was getting involved. Her body language was obvious. He could see her distress.

They were working outside—a hygienic option when the weather was good. It took a long time to get a room clean, and outside the rain periodically cleaned things up. He was sitting at a table and chairs they'd brought themselves. That was his surgery.

Gina didn't even have that. She was sitting on the grass twenty yards from where he was sitting. He couldn't hear what she was saying, but that they were talking through last night's accident was obvious.

She'd be expecting him to do something. She'd be judging…

No.

She didn't expect anything, he reminded himself. She was going home the day after tomorrow and he didn't have to answer to her. He had nothing to do with her.

Together they had a son.

'Will I have a scar?' Chris demanded, and Cal thought if he wasn't careful, yes, he would have.

'It's not too deep.'

'I don't mind having a scar.'

'I can count six already. That's enough for any kid.'

'Men have scars.'

'Only if they live long enough to be men,' Cal told him. 'Which you won't if you keep sniffing petrol and fighting with glass. Scars in the tribe you come from are supposed to be a sign of wisdom. There's not much wisdom in a scar like this.'

'No,' Chris admitted, and he cast a shamefaced glance behind him at his mate. 'I got a bit scared when Aaron bled. And…' He swallowed. 'I don't like it that they all got killed last night. I reckon they'd been sniffing petrol, too.'

'So stop it,' Cal said gently.

'There's nothing else to do.'

Gina was rising now. She still had her arm round the old lady's shoulders. Mary was weeping, Cal saw, and Gina's face was creased in concern. Gina was upset.

She didn't know these people. She didn't have to get involved.

Neither did he.

Gina looked across at him and gave him a half-smile, as if she expected that he share her distress.

'You need a swimming pool,' Cal said, and where the words had come from he didn't know. But he knew where the idea had come from. Something he'd heard on the radio—something he'd heard happening at a remote settlement a thousand miles from here and had thought a great plan.

Someone who might get involved might grab a plan like that and run with it.

'A swimming pool.' Aaron and Chris were looking at him like he was stupid.

'That's right,' he said, and it was too late to retract now. 'It's fifty miles to the coast from here, and even then you can't swim during the hot six months. Too many stingers. You guys need a pool.'

'Yeah, but how would we get a swimming pool?' Aaron demanded. Cal had been dressing Chris's leg while he spoke and now he motioned to Aaron to take his friend's place in front of him. Aaron's face had a long, vicious scratch. It didn't need stitching as Chris's leg had, but it needed to be scrupulously cleaned if it wasn't to be infected. Cal started work with care but the boys' attention was caught.

'You mean one of those paddling pools you blow up,' Aaron said scornfully. 'We had one. It lasted a whole day and a half before it got a hole in it.'

Gina was in earshot now. She was walking Mary over to see him, Cal realised, and he wished he could stop this conversation now, but both boys were staring at him in half-resentful expectation that this was nothing. It was definitely too late to back out.

'If I could talk the politicians into building a swimming pool here, would you guys go to school?'

'Nah,' Chris said scornfully. 'Why would we?'

'Because Mr Robbins and Mrs Cook run classes every day here, and they never have any more than six or so kids. They have heaps of room, they're great people, and if you guys learn to read and write then there's so much you could do.'

'Like what?' Chris demanded.'

'Well, you could get put up for selection for the national footy teams for one thing,' Cal said. 'They won't look at you unless you can read.'

'Yeah, but that's not till we're sixteen,' Chris objected. 'We might be dead before then.'

Which was the absolute truth, Cal thought grimly. It was even a probability.

OK.

OK, what?

Gina was watching him now. His conscience. And back at home was a little boy who looked like him—whose very existence seemed to make him aware that he ought to be doing more

He had to get involved. Just a bit.

'I'm going to work on getting you guys a swimming pool,' he told them.

They stared at him, disbelieving.

'You gotta be joking.'

'I'm not joking.' He glanced up at Gina but his eyes were caught instead by the little lady she was holding. Mary's face was swollen with weeping but her eyes were arrested. Her face was still. Waiting.

What was he doing? He didn't get involved.

He was involved.

'I was reading about a place like this near Darwin,' he told them, thinking it through as he talked. 'The locals started a collection, they got a government grant to help and they've built a swimming pool. They feed it from an underground bore. There's bore water here.'

'No one would do that for us,' one of the boys muttered.

'If they did it there I don't know why they wouldn't do it here,' Cal said. 'All it needs is some pressure.'

'No one here'd be a leader enough to put pressure on anyone,' Mary said slowly, and the old woman's voice was husky from weeping. 'We're so…' She searched for an appropriate word and didn't find one. 'Stuffed,' she said at last. 'Finished. We keep getting hit and the more we're hit the more we can't get up again. Now…all our young 'uns are dead…'

'Not all your young 'uns,' Cal said gently. He was clearing every trace of dirt and broken glass from Aaron's face. 'I'm so sorry about last night. But there's kids left and we need to move forward for them. We need desperately to move forward. I'm prepared to fight on your behalf.'

'You,' the old woman said, and Cal grimaced inside. He'd been coming out to this settlement for years, and until now he'd never got personally involved. It was no wonder the woman's tone was incredulous.

'Yeah, me,' he said ruefully, and tried not to look at Gina—who was looking as incredulous as the old lady. 'It's not only a way to give you some pleasure, but it's a way to get the kids to go to school.'

'How?' Aaron said belligerently.

'Stay still,' Cal told him, and Gina moved in to help, cutting a dressing to size so he had it ready as soon as the antiseptic was in place.

'Easy,' Cal said. 'Once we get the pool, there'd be a rule in place. If you miss a day's school without a very good reason, you'd be excluded from the pool for a month.'

'You're kidding me,' Aaron said. 'That's not fair.'

'That'd make 'em go to school,' the old lady said, thinking it through. Deflected for a moment from her tragedy. 'It's so hot and dusty here all the time, and the kids are bored stupid, and if they got to stay outside a fence, watching other kids swim…'

'Not fair,' Aaron said again, and Cal grinned.

'Fair or not, you'd go to school.'

'It'd be a start,' Gina said, and he glanced at her and glanced away again. Fast.

He wasn't doing this for her. He wasn't.

'You say you'd get it going?' Mary whispered, and he nodded.

'I'll come out next week and we'll have a community meeting. Next Wednesday?'

'So soon?'

'It might help,' he said diffidently. 'You need it, Mary.'

'Mary has been having what seem like panic attacks,' Gina told him. 'I thought maybe we could give her a script for something to help over the next few days.'

'There's no need,' Mary muttered, and she fixed Cal with a look that said now he'd offered there was no way he could back down. 'I couldn't see a way past this mess we're in. Now, though...a pool... If you really think it's possible...'

'I do.'

'Then I don't want no tranquillisers,' she told him. 'I just want a plan forward.'

'Do you mean it?'

They were in the car, headed back toward Crocodile Creek, and Gina was looking at him as if he'd grown another head.

'Of course I mean it.'

'You'd build a swimming pool out here.'

'It's possible,' he said, and he knew he sounded defensive but he couldn't help it. 'I've been thinking about it ever since I read about the other place. It seemed such a good idea. How to bribe kids to go to school in one easy hit.'

'And you'll get the money? These people don't look like they have anything.'

'I might have a route through Charles,' he told her.

She frowned. 'Charles is rich?'

'Charles's family is rich. The Wetherby station is vast. Old man Wetherby was a nasty piece of work. After Charles's accident he couldn't bear looking at him. Disability disgusted him. That seemed fine by Charles—he couldn't stand the old man either. Anyway Philip, Charles's brother, now runs the place. Charles refused to take anything personally from the farm but he's not above touching his brother's conscience when he needs something for the hospital. Or in this case, if he needs something toward a pool. Philip can well afford it.'

'But will he?'

'There are things going on between Charles and his brother that I don't understand,' Cal told her. 'All I know is that Philip is a weak reed but an incredibly rich weak reed, and a contribution for a pool wouldn't touch his huge financial base. As long as he doesn't have to commit any effort…'

'It'll be you who has to commit the effort.'

'So it seems.'

'Why are you doing this?' she said, so softly he hardly heard.

Why was he doing this? Good question. 'It has to be done,' he said, trying to figure it out for himself. 'Those kids last night shouldn't have died.'

'No, but they're just more in a long sequence of tragedies. Mary was telling me. The death rate among the adolescents out here is horrific.'

'So it is.'

'So why today?' she whispered 'Why today did you get out of your comfort zone and offer to do something about it?'

'I don't know.' And wasn't that the truth?

'Was it because of me?'

'Gina…'

'Because I accused you of not letting yourself care?'

'I care.'

'Of course you care,' she told him. 'You care and you care, even when you try so hard not to. It's impossible not to care, Cal. It's impossible not to expose yourself to get hurt.'

'Can we do without the life lesson?'

'Sorry.' She relapsed into silence but she still seemed uncomfortable.

'We could still get married,' he said, and she jerked into rigid awareness.

'I beg your pardon.'

'You could stay here. We could marry. I could care for you and CJ.'

'Care…as in look after.'

'Of course.'

'Why would I want you to look after me?'

'Hell, Gina…'

'I might agree if it was mutual,' she told him.

'How do you mean—mutual?'

'Well, if you, for instance, told me that what happened out there today moved you to tears and you felt just dreadful and you needed a hug in order to get the strength you need to keep going.'

He froze.

There was a long silence. Her words played over and over in his head.

It was like there was a huge carrot in front of his nose— no, a wonderful, amazing dream, enticing him, sweetly singing its siren song. All he had to do was take a step forward.

And fall into a chasm so deep he could never get out of it.

He'd fallen before. He couldn't. He just…couldn't. He'd taken one small step today and he hadn't fallen, but this wasn't a small step. This was huge. Vast. Overwhelming.

To admit he needed someone.

He needed Gina.

He didn't. He couldn't.

'No.'

'Of course, no,' she said softly into the stillness. 'Of course, no, Cal Jamieson. So I guess that means we're stuck. You're here working your wonderful medicine—and taking one tiny step into caring that might or might not destroy you. And me returning to Idaho. And never the twain shall meet.'

'If you weren't so pig-headed…'

'Not pig-headed. Sane.'

'Why?'

'Because I've broken my heart over you once before, Cal,' she said steadily. 'I'm not going down that route again.'

'I'm not asking you to break your heart.'

'You think living with you and loving you and watching you not need me for ever and ever and ever would do anything but drive me crazy?' she asked. 'Cal, you're a doctor short in this wonderful hospital of yours, and Hamish's make-do medicine won't cut it. You definitely need a psychiatrist.'

CHAPTER EIGHT

CJ WAS waiting for them when they got back, sitting on the veranda steps, licking the world's biggest ice cream, while Rudolph Mutt sat adoringly at attention beside him. Hamish was watching them, and as they appeared he uncoiled his long legs from the veranda seat and smiled.

CJ was still wearing Bruce's hat.

Tomorrow his son was going to spend his last day in Australia with the man who had given him the hat, Cal thought.

Not him.

'Here they are, CJ,' Hamish was saying. 'The world's best medical team, home from sorting out the problems of the world.'

'How are things here?' Cal wasn't in the mood for smiling. He was feeling like things were out of his control and he wasn't sure how to get them back.

Hamish's smile faded. 'We've had the coroner working through the autopsies, and one of the kids' dads has had a heart attack.' He hesitated. 'Gina, we were wondering whether you'd see him. You looked after the prawn fisherman last night...'

'He just had indigestion,' she said. 'It didn't take a cardiologist to work that out.'

'Yeah, it was a pity we had to take the chopper two hundred miles out to sea when all he needed was antacid.' He hesitated. 'But this guy's a definite case. Charles wants to send him down to Cairns but he won't go. And maybe I wouldn't either if I had a kid to bury.'

'I'll see him,' Gina said. CJ had risen for a hug and she was hugging him, hard—ice cream and all—and that was doing something really strange to Cal's insides.

Damn, he wanted to be in that hug.

No, he didn't. What was he thinking?

'Our baby?' Gina asked, her face muffled by small boy. 'Lucky?'

'Lucky's good,' Hamish told her. 'His heart rate's settled beautifully. A couple of minor prem hassles but I'm thinking he's no more than three weeks early. We have him on oxygen but it's more a precaution than a necessity.' He eyed Cal and then stooped to pat Rudolph. 'We might be seeing a happy ending with Lucky.'

'The von Willebrand's?'

'Tests came back positive,' Hamish told them. 'It's a hassle but properly treated it should be no more than a minor inconvenience as he goes through life. And it does mean we called it right in not giving him heparin now.'

'What of his mother?' Cal asked.

'No news. Harry has every cop in the state looking for her, and every medical clinic within a thousand miles. I told him about the von Willebrand's thing and he's scared we have a bleeder.' He stooped and hugged the dog as if he needed some comfort himself. 'I guess we all are.'

'I'm not sure. I'm guessing it may well be the father,' Gina said.

'Why do you say that?'

'I am just guessing. But I saw the birth site. If the mother had been a bleeder as well, there would have been a lot more.'

'Maybe you're right,' Hamish said, relaxing a little. He looked from Gina to Cal and back again and he stopped relaxing. He looked interested. 'So, out at the settlement…bad?'

'Bad,' Cal said.

'Cal's going to organise them a swimming pool,' Gina told him, still hugging CJ, and Hamish stared.

'The hell you are.'

'Yeah, well, I'm going to take a shower first,' Cal said, and tried to push past him to go into the house, but his friend blocked the way.

'You're going to organise them a swimming pool?'

'To bribe the kids to go to school.' Gina smiled. 'It sounds a fantastic idea.'

'I read about that,' Hamish said. 'I remember showing Emily and saying what a great idea. And Em said what we needed was someone to get enthusiastic and organise it here.'

'Cal's enthusiastic.'

'Not now I'm not,' Cal said. 'I'm not the least bit enthusiastic. Hamish, move over, mate. I want to get past.'

'When I've finished asking questions,' Hamish told him. 'So you're going to organise a pool.' He glanced across at Gina. 'And you're going to help?'

'Not me. I'm going back to the US.'

'I don't understand,' Hamish complained. 'No one's making sense.'

'My ice cream's squashed,' CJ told them all conversationally. He pulled back from his hug and eyed his mother's cleavage. 'I think some of my ice cream's dropped down there.'

'Great,' said Gina. She peered down. 'Oh, goody. Chocolate.'

'I guess that means you get first crack at the shower,' Hamish told her, and grinned. 'Want some help?'

'CJ will help,' she said with dignity.

'I was offering Cal's services.'

'Butt out, Hamish.' Cal was feeling like so many things

were being thrown at him his head was spinning. He needed space. He needed to get away by himself and sort his head out. And the chocolate ice cream had gone *where*?

'Will you look after my dog?' CJ was asking him, and he tried to think of something useful to say. Hamish was chuckling.

'Hamish is a paediatrician,' he told CJ. 'He's good at handling babies. Rudolph is a puppy and therefore—'

'CJ, Rudolph isn't your dog,' Gina told her son, tugging him up the steps.

'The Grubbs can't keep him,' CJ said, distressed. 'He has to be my dog.'

'We can't take him home, honey.'

'I'm going back to the hospital,' Hamish said. 'I'm needed.' He gave them his most virtuous look and disappeared. Fast. Before he ended up with a dog.

'I need to keep Rudolph,' CJ said urgently, not even noticing Hamish's exit in his distress. 'What will happen to him if I can't keep him?'

'Cal will look after him,' Gina said, 'Won't you, Cal?'

'I don't want a dog.'

'Of course you do,' she told him. 'Everyone wants a dog and he's splendid. You won't have to need him at all.'

'What's that supposed to mean?'

'Figure it out, Einstein.' She tempered the words with a smile but the smile was strained. 'He's a fine dog, Cal. You offered to take us because you thought we needed you, but we don't. But Rudolph needs a home and CJ needs to know that he's in good hands.'

'But…' Cal stared down at Rudolph. He really was the weirdest mutt. His huge, long face looked lugubrious already and he was only a pup. Imagine what he'd look like when it got some age on.

The dog was staring right up at Cal and suddenly the

bounce had gone right out of him. He expected to be kicked. His tail was right underneath him and he whimpered.

'See. He knows his life hangs in the balance,' Gina said.

'What are you looking at me like that for?' Cal demanded of the dog. 'The Grubbs aren't planning on putting you down.'

'What's putting down?' CJ asked, and Cal knew he was lost.

'Fine,' he said. 'Fine,' he told the dog. 'I'll keep him,' he told Gina. 'You walk back into my life and suddenly I'm organising swimming pools and taking care of manipulative dogs and…'

'And what, Cal?' She tilted her chin and met his look with one of defiance.

'And nothing.'

'That's what I thought,' she whispered. 'Nothing. CJ and I are off to have a shower and then I have patients to see. You have a dog to care for and a swimming pool to organise. Separate lives, Cal. But that's the way you want it. Isn't it?'

'And the damnable thing is that I now have the Grubbs' dog, which they've been trying to palm off onto unsuspecting victims for the last two months and they didn't even try me, and now look!' Cal was in Charles's office, and Rudolph was beside him. The mutt had cheered right up. He was leaning—hard—against Cal's leg and his tail was sweeping the carpet as if he'd found paradise.

'He looks quite a nice…personality,' Charles said cautiously, and Cal grimaced.

'If you grin, I'm going to have to slug you.'

'Hey, I'm in a wheelchair.'

'I'll tip you out of the wheelchair and then I'll slug you.' Charles grinned.

'You know, it's not such a bad thing,' he told him. 'You need someone to love and Rudolph sure looks like he needs someone to love,'

'I do not need someone to love.'

'Which is why you're sending Gina home.'

'I'm not sending Gina home either,' Cal snapped. 'I offered to marry her.'

Charles stilled. 'You did what?'

'I offered to marry her. She refused.'

'You offered to marry her,' Charles said cautiously. 'Gee, that was noble of you.'

'It was not noble. And she refused.'

'Why?'

'How would I know?'

'Did you tell her you love her?'

'Yes!'

'You're kidding.' Charles was still staring at Rudolph, who had rubbed against Cal so hard that Cal had put his hand down to push him away. Now, though, the hand had become a scratching post. Cal's fingers were running along the dog's spine and Rudolph was arching in ecstasy. 'I don't believe it.'

'I've never loved anyone else.'

'No,' Charles said cautiously. 'Maybe that's the trouble.'

'Look, it's academic anyway,' Cal told him. 'She's going home to the States the day after tomorrow. Our baby's looking good. Gina could leave tomorrow but apparently she's got some date with Bruce, crocodile hunting.'

'So your son's last day in Australia will be spent with someone else,' Charles said, still carefully watching the dog. 'You know, if you want tomorrow off, we'll cover for you.'

'You know you can't. We're so short-staffed.'

'I see it as an imperative,' Charles said, and he did look at Cal then. 'You have a son, Cal. A son. Do you know how fantastic that is?' His voice was rough with longing and there was a loaded silence. A silence that made Cal rethink. Charles wore his disability lightly but there was suddenly such pain on his face that Cal knew a nerve had been hit.

'I'm sorry, Charles,' he said at last, and Charles gave a bitter laugh.

'You should be sorry, you lucky sod. I can't have kids, and if you know how much that hurts… But you. You have a son appear out of the blue and you don't make the slightest effort to keep him.'

That was a bit much. 'Hey, Charles, I asked her to marry me,' he protested. 'I want to marry her. She needs me. She's diabetic, a single mum, trying to raise a kid by herself…'

'And that's how you proposed.'

'Of course it is.'

'You're a fool.'

'What?'

'I had a proposal once,' Charles said, the pain on his face replaced by a look of reflection. 'A nurse. Abigail. Abby. I went out with her a few times and we had a ball. I even thought I was in love. And then before I got around to proposing, she proposed for me. She said she wanted to spend the rest of her life caring for me. That she thought I was really brave, the way I faced life, and I had so much courage and she'd never let anything hurt me again. She said she loved me. And you know what? I ran a mile.'

Cal stilled. 'You're saying…'

'I'm saying need's no basis for a marriage. If ever I fall for anyone, it will have be someone who needs me as much as I need her. Do you see that, Cal?'

'Yeah, but—'

'But you won't let yourself go there. Because of your past.'

'You know, I really should get myself my own house,' Cal said, raking his hair in disbelief. 'You and Hamish and Emily and Grace. And who else? Even Mrs Grubb's had a go at me. Let's sort out Cal's problems.'

'Well, you won't sort them out yourself.'

'I don't have any problems.'

'Yeah, you do. You have a kid out there who's desperate for a dad, and you have a fantastic woman who you've held in your heart for years...'

'I don't need her.'

'The household says you do,' Charles said with a wry grin. 'And who are you to go against the decision of your house-mates? You'd be a very brave man to try. Now, tell me about this planned swimming pool of yours. Hamish says you need Wetherby money. How are we going to organise that?'

She should have organised to leave tomorrow, Gina thought over and over again as the night stretched out. She was lying in bed and she could hear people out in the living room. They were playing billiards. Cal was there. She could hear his voice, raised in protest at something Hamish was saying, laughing with Emily, and there was such a surge of longing in her heart that it was all she could do not to get up and join them.

Did they know how lucky they were—to have such friends?

She'd told Cal she was going home to Idaho to her family and friends, but in truth her family and her friends were few and far between. Paul's illness had isolated them. Friends had dropped away and Paul's mother had died. Gina's parents were divorced and remarried with more children and grand-children, and Gina was only a tiny part of their lives.

The laughter from the living room was unbearable.

Maybe she should marry Cal, she thought bleakly. It'd be better than going back to Idaho. And maybe it could work. Maybe in time...

Maybe in time she'd break her heart. To love with Cal but to never be allowed close. To always be the taker. The depen-dent one.

No.

So she should leave now.

But she'd thought the baby might need her and so she'd promised to stay and now she'd told Bruce she'd come with him on his crocodile-hunting expedition, and she'd told CJ and he was wearing Bruce's hat and he was so excited…

Bruce was definitely interested.

So what? She wasn't interested. Not while Cal was alive in the world.

It was an impossible situation. Crazy.

One more day. One day spent hunting crocodiles and then it would be over.

It would never be over and she knew it.

Midnight. Cal was staring down at Lucky's incubator, watching the tiny chest rise and fall. Over and over. One tiny baby taking the first step toward living.

He slipped his hand through an incubator port and touched the tiny hand. The little fist opened and the fingers clung around his finger.

'He's fantastic.'

He was startled but he didn't jerk. Not with that tiny hand holding him with such trust. It was Emily coming up behind him.

'Your dog's blocking the entrance to Casualty,' Emily told him. 'I thought I'd find you here.'

'He's not my dog.'

'CJ says he is,' Emily said, and smiled. She looked down at the baby and her smile faded. 'Poor little one.'

'He'll live.'

'But where's his mother? His family? He has no one.'

'He's tough,' Cal said, trying not to let the sensation of one tiny hand clutching his finger make him sound emotional. 'He's a survivor. You don't need people to survive.'

'Of course you do,' Emily said, startled. 'We need to find him a foster-family. They'll have to be the best. Special people to love a special little boy.'

'He'll survive,' Cal said again into the stillness, and Em shook her head.

'There's survival and survival, Cal. We need to find this little one someone who'll love him to bits.' She smiled. 'What about you?'

'Me?'

'Well, you're in adoption mode. First Rudolph and now…'

'Don't be ridiculous.'

'I'm not being ridiculous,' she said thoughtfully. 'If you can't have CJ…well, I think a son is just who you need.'

'I don't need anyone.'

'Now, why do I think that's a nonsense?' she said. She watched as he reluctantly released the grip of those tiny fingers. 'Why are you here?'

'I thought I'd check—'

'Hamish and I are well able to look after him and Gina's only a call away.'

'I thought—'

'You thought your bedroom seemed really, really empty,' Emily said softly. 'Well, mine is, too. It's a really bleak feeling but it's something we're going to have to get used to. Meanwhile, can I suggest you go remove your mutt from the door of Casualty before someone falls over him and sues the hospital for zillions? We've all had just about as much drama as we can stand in the last few days—and then some.'

'She won't talk to me. She's got her head in the pillow and she won't even look up when I go in.' Jim sounded as shaken as his daughter and Honey pulled out a kitchen chair and motioned him into it.

'Hush. You're not to upset yourself.'

'But what's going on?'

'She's menstrual and she has the flu,' Honey told him. Then because he clearly wasn't satisfied she added a rider. 'And

she's been thinking of the boy you sent away. Dwelling on it. What she needs is something to take her mind off it but it's a bit hard where we are.'

'Why is she thinking about him now?' Jim was astounded. 'I thought she'd forgotten all about him.'

'When you're feeling poorly, things mount up in your head.'

'That's why she won't talk to me. She blames me.'

'She knows why you hate the Wetherbys,' Honey told him. 'We all do. She doesn't blame you. It was just unfortunate. For her to fall for him...'

'Then why isn't she talking to me?'

'She's not talking to anyone,' Honey said miserably. 'I guess we have to sit back and wait for her to get better. All by herself.'

Breakfast at the house was very, very strained. There were six medics sitting around the breakfast table. The huge toaster on the sideboard was working overtime; they were onto their second pot of marmalade but there wasn't a lot of conversation. Everyone was watching Gina and Cal—and Gina and Cal were very carefully trying not to look at each other.

How had Cal lived in this house for so long under these watchful eyes? Gina thought. Friends or not, she'd have gone nuts.

'Why isn't anyone talking?' CJ demanded through toast, and Gina ruffled his curls—more a reassurance to herself than a reassurance to CJ.

'They're all busy eating,' she said, 'I expect they'll start talking when they finish their toast.'

There was a general regroup. Talk started.

'The weather's looking good,' Emily said, and they all nodded.

'You don't call scorching hot and no rain in sight good, do you?' Hamish demanded. 'I want to go back to Scotland.'

'Are you hunting crocodiles today, CJ?' Emily asked with a desperate look at Hamish, as if she was pleading for support.

'Yes,' CJ said, adjusting his hat and swelling a little with importance. 'We are.'

'You could go, too, couldn't you, Cal?' Emily asked brightly, and everyone at the table looked at Cal.

'That's dumb,' Cal snapped. 'You know how short-staffed we are.'

'Just a thought,' Em said.

'Is Rudolph going?' Hamish asked.

'Rudolph isn't my dog any more,' CJ said mournfully. 'He's Cal's dog.'

'I wouldn't be the least bit surprised if Cal offered to lend him to you,' Hamish told him.

'Hamish!' Em said, shocked. 'You know they've only had one day together so far. Cal and Rudolph need to bond. And, besides, dogs are crocodile bait.'

'Maybe I could lend him…' Cal started, but got such a glare from Gina for his pains that he backed off.

Good, Gina thought. Back in your box, buster. And don't come out till I'm gone.

'You're sure you're happy for me to go today?' she said, addressing herself solely to Hamish. 'If you're the least bit worried about Lucky…'

'Lucky's fine,' Hamish said. 'Isn't he, Emily? Emily's been up half the night with him.'

'Why?' Gina frowned. 'I thought he was settled.'

'He is,' Hamish told her. 'But there's a lot of people in this place who don't seem to be sleeping. Isn't that so, Mike? Emily? Cal?' No answer.

'Mr Narmdoo's stable,' Gina said, to no one in particular. 'He's pain-free this morning. The ECG changes are settling and cardiac enzymes are only minimally raised. It seems to have been a relatively minor infarct, but he's going to need follow-up. Angiography will show whether he needs bypass surgery.'

'He won't have it even if he needs it,' Hamish told her. 'Most of the people from the settlement refuse to go to the city. That's why we had Simon…' He paused and looked at Em. 'Um. Simon was our cardiologist.'

'He may come back,' Em said stoutly. 'He just…needed to go.'

'If he doesn't then we're in trouble,' Hamish told her. 'A cardiologist and a surgeon—like, for instance, you and Cal— can save a lot of lives up here.'

'I think I hear Bruce,' Gina said abruptly, and rose from the table. 'Coming, CJ?'

'I haven't finished my toast.'

'I'll meet you on the veranda,' Gina told him. 'It's getting a bit hot in here.'

Cal watched them go from the veranda.

Gina and CJ and Bruce the crocodile hunter.

'We can manage without you.' Charles was right beside him and he swore.

'One day you'll give me a heart attack.'

'Then you'll need a cardiologist.'

'Leave it, Charles.'

'I'm serious,' Charles told him. 'Miraculous as it seems, everything here seems quiet. If you want to go croc hunting with your son…'

'Charles, leave it.'

'He is your son, Cal. He's going back to the States tomorrow.'

'I don't need a family,' Cal growled.

'You're a fool, then,' Charles said cheerfully. 'You know, if that was my son, if that was my woman…'

'They're not.'

'They'll find someone else.' They watched as Bruce solicitously helped Gina into his ancient croc-spotting truck. 'Maybe they already have.'

'What, Bruce?'

'He may not look much, but his tours are earning him a fortune. He has twenty guides on the payroll now. And you have to admit he's good-looking.'

'The people Gina loves are in Idaho,' Cal said, but there was a trace of uncertainty in his voice.

Charles looked up at his friend's face and his own face grew thoughtful.

'Things change,' he murmured. 'People change.'

'Not me.'

'Then you're a fool.'

CHAPTER NINE

WHAT was she doing out on a river, looking for crocodiles, when it was her last day ever close to Cal?

He didn't want her.

Gina sat in the bow of the boat and listened to Bruce chat to CJ about the mating habits of crocodiles. Bruce really was a nice person. He had three other tourists in the boat, an American couple and their teenage daughter, and he was including them all in his chat. He was making them laugh, making sure they all had fun.

He was very interested in her.

She knew it. She knew it in the way he watched her, the way he touched her.

She wasn't the least bit interested.

Cal…

He had to unbend. He had to.

He wasn't.

She was going home.

The day stretched on. It was the quietest of days, there was no trauma at all.

Cal was almost longing for the radio to burst into life, bringing action, bringing something to keep his thoughts occupied.

Nothing.

In the nursery Em was sitting by Lucky's incubator and he knew she was feeling exactly as he was.

'He doesn't need specialling,' he said gently, and Em flashed him a look of anger.

'He needs someone to love him.'

'We'll find his mother.'

'Yeah, right. And meanwhile I'll love him for her.'

She'd fallen for Simon, he thought bleakly. This was the consequence.

Gina would never treat him as Simon had treated Em.

Cut it out.

Jill was in the nurses' station. Rigid, uncommunicative Jill, who took her job as director of nursing with all care but as little humour as possible. He walked in to look up patient notes before doing a ward round, and she met him with a rueful smile.

'This place is like a tomb.'

This, from Jill? Things must be really bad.

'Too much has happened too fast,' he said softly. 'All these deaths. And Simon and Kirsty…'

'Em still doesn't believe he's not coming back. Even though Kirsty told Mike what the situation was.'

'I think she knows in her heart,' Cal said. 'She's hurting.'

'And how about you, Cal? Are you hurting?'

He sighed, dug his hands into the pockets of his coat and glowered. 'Jill, I thought I could depend on you to butt out of what's not your business.'

'It's my business if everyone in my hospital is going around with a face as mournful as that stupid dog of yours. Speaking of which, Rudolph is now draped across the entrance to the kitchen. Will you ask him to move?'

'Sure.' A marrow bone should do it, he thought. He and Rudolph had rather enjoyed sitting on the back step and communing over a marrow bone at three that morning.

She eyed him with caution. 'So you're going to keep him?'

'CJ wants me to.'

'CJ won't know anything about it when he goes back to the States.'

'Jill?'

'Yes?'

'Leave it.'

'Sure,' she said, and smiled, which for Jill was unusual all by itself. 'I'll leave it. But do cheer up.' She shoved a clipboard at him. 'This'll help.'

He stared down at the name on the chart. Albert Narmdoo. Mild coronary. Father of one of the boys who'd died.

'Right,' he said. 'Great. What's happening?'

'Nothing.'

He raised his brows in query.

'Just nothing,' Jill repeated. 'He's not eating. He's just staring at the ceiling. His wife came in this morning and the rest of his kids, but he didn't even speak to them. He's just…lost.'

His heart sank. 'I'll see what I can do.'

'Of course you will,' she told him. And then, before he could begin to imagine what was coming, she leaned forward and hugged him. Jill. Hugging. Unbelievable.

'Go on, Cal,' she said softly. 'Let go. There's a life out there, just waiting.'

As Jill had said, Albert was motionless. He was a big man, one of the elders of his community, his skin so dark his face seemed almost a chasm on the pure white pillows.

Cal walked forward and touched him on the shoulder, but the man didn't register.

'Albert?'

Albert turned eyes that were dulled with pain toward him, and the pain behind them made Cal's heart wrench in pity. 'The kids say you're going to build us a swimming pool,' he whispered.

'I'm going to try.'

'Won't bring…anyone back.'

One of the hardest parts of the indigenous culture was the rigid rule that the names of the dead were no longer spoken. Cal gripped Al's shoulder and watched the agony on his face, and thought they should be able to speak of his son.

He was right. This was what loving was all about, he thought bleakly. Loss. He watched the raw pain on Albert's face and he thought, no, he was right, it was better to do as he'd learned to do. Not to love…

But as if he'd spoken the words out loud, the man reached up and gripped his hand. Hard.

'I've had so much,' he whispered. 'Six kids. Six kids and their mother, and this is the first I've lost. It wrenches you apart, losing, but I've been lying here thinking what if I hadn't had him. You know, when I was a young 'un I didn't want any of it. I wanted to be by myself.'

'You would have missed out,' Cal said, seeing where Albert was headed, seeing where he wanted to head.

'Too right I would have missed out.' His face twisted. 'You know, two days ago, me and…well, we went outback to where we buried his grandfather. Spent the night out there. We woke at dawn and we sat and watched the sun rise over the ranges, just him and me…and it was…well, it was worth everything. And now there's death and my ticker's playing up and maybe it won't be long for me either, but that moment… Hell, to have lost that… If I'd had my way and not had him…' There were tears streaming down the man's face and he gripped Cal's hand, hard. 'You just grab it, boy,' he told him. 'You just never know…but you just grab it now, 'cos the pain will come regardless, but those moments…no one can take them away from you, ever. Me and my boy, that morning. It'll stay with me for ever and it's my gift and I'll love him for life.'

Enough. He released Cal's hand and he turned his face into

the pillow. Cal stood, motionless, his hand on the man's shoulder. He stood until Al's face eased a little. He checked the chart, he wrote up medication and then he hauled a chair up beside the window and sat.

'No need for you to stay,' Albert said.

'I'd like to, if you don't mind,' Cal said. 'I can see the sea from here.'

'Got your own thinking to do?'

'I have.'

He could go down to the beach and do his thinking, he knew. But he wanted to be here.

He needed company.

He needed…

The afternoon was hot and humid and there were no crocodiles. They drifted slowly down the river. The Americans were talking to Bruce, swapping yarns, intent on outdoing each other in travel tales. CJ had Bruce's binoculars, checking out every floating log, every mound in the mangrove swamps on the riverside. Imagining jaws.

Gina let her mind go blank and she drifted.

Tomorrow she'd leave.

For ever.

She was empty, desolate and she was turned into herself so she didn't hear the boat until it was almost on them. A speedboat, blasting along the river far faster than was legal or safe. A group of people on board with beer cans waved in greeting, yelling, yahooing, blasting past them with a wash of white water in their wake.

Bruce shouted a warning and she swerved around, reaching automatically for CJ. But CJ was rocking, falling. He clutched the side and held on, and she thought he was safe, but his hat, his dratted hat, fell overboard.

With a gasp of distress he was up, leaning over, trying to hold it.

She grabbed for him but the second wave of the speedboat's wake hit, knocking her sideways.

Her hand just touched CJ—just touched, but couldn't hold him. Her fingers closed on thin air and her son was gone.

Cal was in the radio room when the call came through. He'd been sitting with Albert until he'd drifted off to sleep. Longer. He'd sat and stared out the window until he'd lost track of time, until his mind had told him it was time to move forward.

Where to?

He still wasn't sure. He needed to find Gina, he thought, and he went to find Charles first to tell him he needed the rest of the day off. But he walked in the door as the call came.

'Crocodile Creek Rescue Response.' Charles himself was taking the call. 'Harry. What's the problem?'

Harry. The local police sergeant. Maybe they'd found Lucky's mother, Cal thought, and he sent a silent prayer that that was the case.

But it wasn't good news. He watched Charles's face and he knew this was trouble.

'The chopper will be in the air in minutes,' he snapped. 'Hell, Harry, you know that river…'

But the line was already dead. Whatever was happening, Harry was moving fast.

Charles spun round. Then he saw Cal and his face froze.

'You.' And something about the way he said it…

'What?'

Charles took a deep breath, regrouping. Or trying to regroup.

'Harry's just had a call,' he told him. 'From the northern reaches of Crocodile Creek. Faint call, just about out of range, from an American tourist who's out with Bruce Hammond.'

With Bruce Hammond. The croc hunter who'd taken Gina and CJ out.

'What?' he asked, and his voice sounded disjointed. Strange. Like someone else was speaking, not him.

'It might be nothing,' Charles warned. 'Harry can't get back to them. No one's answering.'

'What?'

'The boy's been washed overboard,' Charles said bleakly. 'That's all we know. CJ's missing.'

It was a ten-minute flight but even so it was the longest flight Cal had ever known. Mike was at the controls. Cal was beside him, straining the machine to go faster, and Hamish was in the back.

'Because I want a doctor there who's not emotionally involved,' Charles had said.

'Don't send me, then,' Hamish had said. 'I'm emotionally involved.'

'Just go, the lot of you,' Charles had snapped. 'And bring CJ home.'

Charles was emotionally involved himself. CJ had been at the base for a whole two days and already he'd wriggled his way into everyone's heart.

Bring CJ home. The words rang over and over in Cal's head. Home.

Home was here. Home was with him. He had to find him. He had to bring CJ back to Crocodile Creek. They needed to stay here. They needed…

It wasn't working. The line he'd been using all this time to try and persuade Gina to stay was ringing hollow. CJ might well not need him at all.

His son might be dead.

The vision of the bereft Albert slammed back into his heart and stayed there.

You just grab it now, 'cos the pain will come regardless, but those moments…no one can take them away from you, ever. Me and my boy, that morning. It'll stay with me for ever and it's my gift and I'll love him for life.

What had *he* had? Cal thought grimly. One bedtime. He'd read his son one story and now he was gone.

One story was never going to be enough. He wanted more. He wanted so much.

He needed his son.

He needed Gina.

He sat rigid in the helicopter with Mike staring grim-faced ahead, and Cal did his own staring ahead.

What a fool he'd been. What a stupid, hopeless, inadequate fool. So many people had tried to tell him, but he'd done it his way. He'd tried to make himself self-contained, but to do that…it was just plain dumb. He could share his life with Gina and with CJ and with Rudolph and whoever else came along, and he could love them to bits and he could let himself need them, and why not? Because whatever disaster happened in the future, he could never feel any worse than he did right now.

'For God's sake, how much longer?' he exploded, and Mike glanced across with sympathy.

'Five minutes, mate.'

'And there's no news.' Why was the radio dead?

'You know there's transmission dead spots on this part of the river.'

'Then they should move to where they can transmit.'

And move away from where CJ had fallen in? It was a dumb suggestion. Both of them knew it and Mike was kind enough not to say it.

'I'll kill him,' Cal was saying, directing impotent fury at the absent Bruce. 'To take my kid on that part of the river…'

'It's safe enough. They were in a high-sided boat.'

'He should have roped him in.'

'Yeah, I can see CJ agreeing to that,' Mike retorted. 'No one gets roped into tourist boats. There's usually no need. How he fell…'

'Can't you make this machine go faster?'

'We're almost there,' Mike told him, and the big chopper swooped down in a long, low dive. They'd reached the fork where the main tributary turned northwards. 'We're assuming they're on the main branch. Let's just keep our eyes peeled until we see them.'

There was no need for him to say it.

Three pairs of eyes were scouring every inch of the river. With dread.

Gina heard the chopper first. She glanced over her shoulder and she could just make it out, low on the horizon and half-hidden by the canopy of the boat.

'That's the Rescue Response helicopter,' she said, and everyone turned.

'There must be another drama along here somewhere,' Bruce muttered. He was sounding a bit shaken, as indeed they all were. 'It'll be that blasted boat, come to grief. They come here doing ten times the legal limit—they'll have hit a log. They'll be lucky if they haven't killed themselves, the fools.'

'Oh, no,' Gina whispered, hugging CJ closer. His wet little body was dripping against her, making them both soggy, but she didn't care. He was still tear-stained and shaking against her, but the worst of his sobs had died. 'We don't need any more drama.'

But the corpulent American in the back of the boat was suddenly looking uncomfortable.

'We might…we might just have a problem here,' he admitted.

'What?' Bruce raked his bare head and looked exasperated. His expedition to show Gina the river wasn't going to plan.

He hadn't wanted to bring tourists but the Americans were wealthy and prepared to pay a premium if he took them today, so he'd thought he could include them. Now this had happened, and he'd like to be comforting Gina, but he still had to be a tour operator. And on top of everything else, he'd lost his favourite hat!

'When the little guy fell overboard…' the man said.

'Yeah?'

'Well, everyone was screaming and you guys were real busy trying to haul him in and then Marsha screamed about the crocodile and I saw it and I just… I just…' He lifted his cellphone and looked sheepish. 'I knew your emergency code here was 000 so I dialled it.'

'You dialled the emergency services,' Harry said slowly.

'Well, I did.' The man beamed, recovering. 'And, of course, after we got the kiddy back…after seeing those great jaws chomp on that hat…but we had him safe… Well, I guess I clean forgot that I'd phoned, but I'd imagine that's why they're coming, to look for us.'

'I guess they are,' Gina said, and all of a sudden she cheered right up.

The sight of CJ floating downstream on a log, and then the huge teeth rearing up and snapping down on Bruce's hat wasn't something she'd forget in a hurry. She was holding CJ tight and he was still shaking, and she'd been thinking she badly wanted to go home. But suddenly the helicopter was overhead and she thought maybe, just maybe, home was coming to her.

Don't hope, she told herself. It wouldn't be. It wouldn't…

But Bruce was winding the canopy back so they could see up, and the helicopter was right above them, the whirling of its rotor blades causing white water. She could see…

Cal.

He was looking down at her and his face—dear God, his face.

What had he thought?

She knew exactly what he'd thought. The expression on his face matched how she'd felt as she'd seen CJ slide overboard.

Well, why wouldn't he look like that?

He was family.

Home had come to her.

CHAPTER TEN

IT TOOK them ages—ten minutes at least—before the boat could reach a place where the helicopter could land. They steered back along the river, and the helicopter stayed with them every inch of the way.

Up in the chopper, the crew were all crowded into the cockpit, probably breaking every safety rule in the book, Gina decided. Mike and Hamish and Cal. They were watching CJ. The moment the little boy had looked up at them and given a tentative, shaken smile and a tiny wave…well, the expression on all of their faces would stay with Gina for ever.

How had she ever thought she could go back to Idaho?

Home was here.

And then they were mooring at a jetty near a picnic ground. The helicopter was landing. Bruce and the tourists were climbing off the boat, but Gina didn't move. She sat still, holding CJ. The vision of the croc coming toward her son was still with her. Her legs weren't moving. She couldn't get her legs to move.

But she didn't need to.

Cal was out of the chopper and running toward them. He was climbing down into the boat, oblivious of the Americans climbing upward onto the jetty, oblivious of Bruce.

He was gathering her into his arms. He was gathering his

son into his arms, and by the way he held her she knew that this man would never let her go again.

'I thought I'd lost you,' he murmured.

'It was CJ who fell.'

'It makes no difference which,' he told her, pressing his lips into her hair. 'You and CJ. My loves. My two loves. I thought I'd lost my family.'

The nursery lights were dim when they returned.

Equanimity restored, CJ had headed to the hospital kitchen to tell Rudolph and Mrs Grubb all about the very exciting adventures of his hat. Hamish and Mike had disappeared to tell everyone the good news—though the radio call to Charles would have done the same thing. Cal and Gina fell behind, but somehow, because it seemed the right thing to do, the obvious thing to do, for this was who had brought them together in the first place, Cal and Gina ended up beside Lucky's crib.

Lucky was the only baby in the nursery, and he certainly had medical attention. Em, Mike, Hamish, Charles, Jill, and now Cal and Gina. They were all there.

'There's nothing wrong?' Gina asked, startled at the mass medical gathering.

'No,' Jill said, and tried to look busy. 'I was just checking Lucky's obs had been done.'

'And I was doing the obs,' Em said.

'And I was checking that Jill had checked that the obs had been done,' Charles said, and grinned.

'Hey, I'm the paediatrician,' Hamish said. 'I'm in charge of all of this. You can't trust underlings these days.'

'And I'm here in a paramedic capacity,' Mike told them, also smiling. 'When there's so many people packed into a small room, there's a risk of crush injuries and fainting. Especially when emotions are running high.' He smiled across at his friends, his brows rising as he noted their linked hands.

'And emotions seem suddenly to be running a notch higher. Well, well.'

Gina blushed and tried to haul her hand away. Cal held it tighter.

'But the baby's OK?'

'Lucky's great,' Jill said, smiling across at the pair of them. 'He's…lucky. And we were just talking…'

'You were talking,' Charles said. 'Well, bossing, more like.'

'I do not boss.'

'Tell me what you were talking about,' Gina said, taking pity on her.

'We thought, seeing as this hospital has been so miserable…'

'We're not miserable,' Cal said, and Gina gave her love a quelling look.

'Shut up, Cal. You were saying?'

'Tonight's been declared a fire night.'

'A fire night?'

'We do it often,' Cal told her, and there was such a smile in his voice that everyone heard it. Everyone saw it. Gina saw every one of their friends register his happiness, and her own joy increased because of it. 'When we need to celebrate or commiserate or patch up a misunderstanding or whatever, we plan a fire night. We gather all the driftwood we can find on the beach and light it, like some sort of great tribal ceremony.'

'Um,' Gina said faintly. 'Don't tell me. You make sacrificial offerings and dance to the sound of didgeridoos, naked apart from three stripes of ochre on each cheek.'

'Hey, I never thought of that,' Hamish said, brightening.

'We barbecue sausages,' Jill said, quelling him with a look. 'Much more civilised.'

'Or prawns,' Mike said, smiling down at their linked hands, 'In times of high celebration we give sausages a miss and we barbecue prawns.'

'I guess we are celebrating tonight,' Em said softly. She put her finger through the access port in the incubator and stroked Lucky's face. 'We've had these awful deaths. We've had such awful…' She paused for a moment. 'Such awful things. But life goes on. CJ's safe, and Lucky's obs are completely normal. He's wonderful. He really has been… Lucky.'

'For more than just himself,' Cal murmured, and Gina looked at her love and smiled.

'He has.'

'He'll be loved to bits,' Em said stoutly. 'We'll find his mum. I know we will. This little one was born to be loved. He's just fine.'

'Everything's fine,' Cal said. 'Everything and everything and everything.'

Megan woke, unsure for a moment where she was. Moonlight was streaming in over her coverlet. The shivering had stopped. Her bed was warm and soft, and for just a moment she felt safe and secure, as if everything was OK.

She'd been dreaming. And what a dream…

She'd been holding her baby. Her little son. She'd leaned down and let her face rest against the soft down of his cheek and she'd smelt the new-baby smell of him. It had been so real it was with her still, a reality in a world that had gone mad.

A reality.

It was real. She could see him clearly, and she could sense that he was loved and cared for and at peace.

Her baby was OK.

She was no true believer. Somewhere along the way Megan had lost what religion she's had, had lost it in despair and bleakness and the sheer desperate grind for survival.

But now…

Her baby was dead, she thought, but her arms still cradled him, her heart still held him.

Her baby was loved.

Her little son...
He was waiting for her. Her tiny boy.
Her baby.

Away from the fire the beach was deserted. The last of the barbecued prawns had been eaten. Hamish was sitting on a mass of driftwood, strumming a guitar and humming something soft and sweet. Maybe dreaming of a girl back in Scotland? CJ and Rudolph had fallen asleep at his feet, a warm and contented bundle of small boy and dog, and when Cal looked queryingly at his friend, Hamish grinned and paused in his strumming long enough to indicate that his friend should go ahead. He'd take over child- and dog-minding duties.

So Cal was free to lead Gina along the beach, out of the pool of light cast by the fire. Out of earshot of their friends.

The night was still and warm. The tide was coming in and Gina and Cal were barefoot, soaking up the cool of the sea between their toes. Soaking up the serenity of the evening. The serenity of certainty—the knowledge that from here they'd move forward together.

'I can't believe I've been so stupid,' Cal said softly. They'd been swinging their hands as they'd wandered toward the headland but now he paused and twisted so he was facing her. 'What you've gone through alone, because of my stupidity...'

'No.' She took his face between her hands and smiled up at him. 'Cal, if five years ago you'd wanted me, if you'd begged me to stay, if you'd wanted CJ as your son, there'd still have been Paul. And Paul was my husband. He was my friend. I've been thinking about it. If that phone call had come to say he'd been injured, and you'd loved me and wanted me, maybe I still would have had to go. And how much harder would it have been?'

'You'd let me off...'

'There's no letting off,' she told him. 'Five years ago you weren't ready for loving and I wasn't free to return that love.'

He thought about that for a moment and still found it unsatisfactory. 'OK, then,' he said, grudgingly. 'But no matter how you look at it, we've still wasted two days.'

'Um…right.'

'I don't want to waste any more time.'

'No.'

'So will you marry me?'

She thought about it.

'There's a few conditions,' she said at last.

'Like what?'

She tried to make her face stern. She tried to keep the loving laughter at bay—the joy from showing in her response. This was important.

'You're never to ask what my insulin levels are,' she managed. 'You'd be my husband, Cal Jamieson, not my doctor. I've already asked Charles if he'll be my physician and he's agreed.'

'But—'

'No negotiation, Cal. I don't need you as my doctor. Take it or leave it.'

'I'll take it.'

'You're never to sleep on the opposite side of the bed.'

He grinned. 'That's a given.'

'You're to tell me when you're worried or when you're sick or when you're frightened.'

'So you get to know my insulin levels but I don't get to know yours?'

'I have the upper hand,' she said serenely. 'It may be the last time it happens so I'm making the most of it. Promise me, Cal.'

'You drive a hard bargain.'

'I know,' she said smugly. 'But it has to start now. So start. Are you worried about anything now?'

'Um…yes.'

'Why?'

'You might not promise to marry me.'

'I have to think up some more conditions.'

'What about loving?' he said softly. 'And needing. If I promise to need you every day of my life, every hour of every day, every moment…if I promise to need you…'

'As much as I need you,' she whispered. 'I don't think that's possible.'

'How can you still need me?'

'My son loves your stupid dog,' she said, and her hands slipped to his waist and tugged him into her. 'CJ loves your dopey dog. I love him and the only way I can get this whole crazy family together is to agree to marry you. So you see…' But she was forced to pause as his lips met hers, and the pause lengthened and lengthened. When finally she managed to speak again her voice had grown breathless. 'So you see,' she whispered. 'I do need you.'

'You'll be my family?'

'Of course I'll be your family,' she said, really, really unsteadily. 'I think I already am. Maybe I've been your family for five long years and you haven't even realised it. Even Paul…'

'I owe Paul,' Cal said, and the laughter suddenly disappeared as he tried to speak of what he'd been thinking. 'Paul was your husband and his death has brought you back to me. But Paul's decision—to face life, to search for what love truly was—was what brought you to me in the first place. He'll always be honoured in our home.'

'Oh, Cal…'

'Will we have more kids?' he asked, and she stared up at him in such astonishment that he leaned back to see what she was thinking.

'What? What's surprising about that?'

'You want to extend our family?'

'Family's good,' he said, tugging her back to him again. 'Family's great. Three days ago I was alone. Now I have you, I have my son and I have a dog. And I was wondering…' He smiled against her hair. 'Gina, if Lucky's parents aren't found…'

'You'd want him?' She could scarcely speak. This was so much how she'd been feeling herself.

'I guess I've learned that love expands to fit all comers,' he whispered. 'Lucky brought you back to me. We could love him. Couldn't we?'

'Of course we could,' she whispered. 'Of course. Oh, Cal…'

'And if we do find his parents…'

'Then we'll just have to work on making our own babies,' she told him. 'How about that for a good idea?'

He didn't answer. And she didn't speak. His kiss was all the response she needed and their kiss lasted a very long time.

'So you'll marry me,' he said at last into the stillness of the night, and she held him close and felt his heartbeat and wondered how he could ever ask that question.

'Of course I will. My heart.'

'Then I guess we should go back to the fire,' he told her.

She glanced along the beach, where their friends, the medics of Crocodile Creek, were clustered together on the warm sand.

'They're waiting,' Cal said.

'Waiting? For what?'

'To know whether you've said yes.'

'Did they know you were going to propose?' Gina demanded, prepared to be indignant, but Cal smiled and hugged her to him, and then chuckled out loud.

'Welcome to Crocodile Creek, Dr Lopez,' he told her. 'Welcome to our extended family. In this town—in this house—there is no such thing as a secret. There's life and laughter and loving and…' He tugged her hard against him and kissed her again, long and sweetly, with the promise of forever in his kiss.

'And the best is yet to come.'

MILLS & BOON®

Live the emotion

Medical
romance™

0306/03b

HER BOSS AND PROTECTOR *by Joanna Neil*

Dr Jade Holbrook's first day in A&E doesn't go as planned. She discovers her landlord, Callum Beresford, is also her new boss! Jade knows she hasn't made a good impression on the handsome consultant, and is aware that he is watching her every move…

A&E DRAMA: Pulses are racing in these fast-paced dramatic stories

THE SURGEON'S CONVENIENT FIANCÉE
by Rebecca Lang

Theatre Nurse Deirdre Warwick is determined that the two children left in her care will have the best life possible. When Dr Shay Melburne enters her life suddenly, Deirdre finds herself falling hopelessly in love with him – and then he offers her a marriage of convenience…but can he offer her his love?

THE SURGEON'S MARRIAGE RESCUE
by Leah Martyn

Adam Westerman is a successful Sydney surgeon and has returned to the Outback to find the beautiful ex-wife he's never managed to forget. Charge nurse Liv Westerman fears Adam has only come for custody of their child. She finds herself hoping that he has come back for both of them…!

On sale 7th April 2006

Available at WHSmith, Tesco, ASDA, Borders, Eason, Sainsbury's and most bookshops

www.millsandboon.co.uk

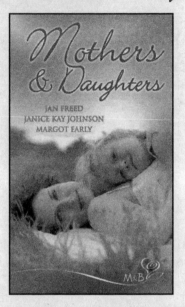

FREE!

4 Books
and a surprise gift!

We would like to take this opportunity to thank you for reading this Mills & Boon® book by offering you the chance to take FOUR more specially selected titles from the Medical Romance™ series absolutely FREE! We're also making this offer to introduce you to the benefits of the Reader Service™—

- ★ **FREE home delivery**
- ★ **FREE gifts and competitions**
- ★ **FREE monthly Newsletter**
- ★ **Exclusive Reader Service offers**
- ★ **Books available before they're in the shops**

Accepting these FREE books and gift places you under no obligation to buy, you may cancel at any time. even after receiving your free shipment. Simply complete your details below and return the entire page to the address below. You don't even need a stamp!

YES! Please send me 4 free Medical Romance books and a surprise gift. I understand that unless you hear from me. I will receive 6 superb new titles every month for just £2.80 each. postage and packing free. I am under no obligation to purchase any books and may cancel my subscription at any time. The free books and gift will be mine to keep in any case.

M6ZEF

Ms/Mrs/Miss/Mr ....Initials.........................

BLOCK CAPITALS PLEASE

Surname...

Address..

....

....Postcode..........................

Send this whole page to:
UK: FREEPOST CN81, Croydon, CR9 3WZ